FALLING FAST

A LAST FRONTIER LODGE NOVEL

J.H. CROIX

This is a work of fiction. Names, characters, businesses, places, events and incidents are either the products of the author's imagination or used in a fictitious manner. Any resemblance to actual persons, living or dead, or actual events is purely coincidental.

Cover by CT Cover Creations

❦ Created with Vellum

DEDICATION

To those who remember what's it's like to learn to love again.

**Sign up for my newsletter for information on new releases &
get a FREE copy of one of my books!**

http://jhcroixauthor.com/subscribe/

Follow me!
jhcroix@jhcroix.com
https://amazon.com/author/jhcroix
https://www.bookbub.com/authors/j-h-croix
https://www.facebook.com/jhcroix

CHAPTER 1

The snow swirled around Ginger Sanders as she raced toward the bottom of the ski slope. A bird flitting through the trees caught her eye and next thing she knew, one of her skis caught on its edge and she lost her balance. For another few seconds, she thought she could stay upright. She managed to slow down as she wobbled. Then, she happened to glance up and see the sexiest man she'd ever laid eyes on a few feet in front of her. Any balance she thought she had was promptly lost. She skidded sideways and landed with a hard thump, coming to a stop beside the skis belonging to the man in question. Her gaze traveled up, up and up until she found herself staring at sex-on-skis.

The ski god looked down at her. Amber eyes with thick lashes met hers. His hair almost matched his eyes, brown gilded with gold. His features were elegant and strong at once, angled cheekbones, a blade of a nose, and a full, sensual mouth. The man's body was well defined under his fitted, high-performance gear—all muscle and nothing else.

As the man knelt down to check on her, Ginger was struck speechless. She'd like to have blamed her tumble in the snow, but truly it was just this man. He sent her brain and her body into a tailspin. She was almost dizzy just looking at him. Which was not good, not good at all. Where the hell did he come from? She'd never laid eyes on him, and she knew most everyone in Diamond Creek, Alaska. He must be a tourist visiting Last Frontier Lodge.

She took a breath and pointlessly ran a hand through her hair as if she could somehow straighten the wild locks damp with snow. The ski god's face came close to hers when he was at her level. Her breath hitched and her pulse took off at a gallop.

"Are you okay?" he asked.

Several beats of silence passed while she simply stared at him. Her cheeks heated when she realized she hadn't managed to answer him. "Um…yeah. I think so." Her words came out in a rapid jumble, the few she'd managed to string together.

The man glanced at her skis, which were resting at an awkward angle in the snow. She moved her legs slightly. Aside from her hip throbbing from where she'd landed on it, she felt okay, although her legs weren't too comfortable with the skis stuck to them.

"Let's get you out of these skis, so you can get your feet under you."

Before she could think, much less form another word, sex-on-skis quickly adjusted her skis and unfastened the bindings. He even carefully slid her skis off. He was not only sexy as hell, but quite helpful—a rather dangerous combination. Still kneeling, he caught her eyes again. "Now that you can move, how are you?"

Ginger stretched her legs out and wiggled them. The cold snow underneath her was starting to seep through her fleece leggings. She looked up into those amber eyes, trying to ignore the electricity zipping through her, and nodded. "I'm, uh… I'm fine."

He held his hand out. Normally, she would have ignored it and clambered up herself, but this man seemed to have practically hypnotized her. His large hand curled around hers and steadily pulled her up. When she was on her feet, she looked up again and tried to gather herself. She couldn't keep acting like a fool who could barely talk.

"Thank you."

She was dying to know who this man was, but she was so flustered, she couldn't seem to say anything else.

His amber eyes held a subtle gleam as he watched her. He reached an arm over and brushed snow off of her shoulders. "You have, uh, a bit of snow on your back," he said, gesturing to her back.

"Oh, oh, right." She pulled her gloves off and shook her coat. As she tried to reach around, she realized she had snow pretty much everywhere, including all over her bottom. She brushed it off and stomped her feet. When she looked up again, she could feel the flush racing up her neck and face. Every look in his eyes flustered her even more.

Shit. Don't blush like an idiot. What the hell is wrong with you? You don't notice men. They are in the no-zone. Get a grip and act normal.

As she was frantically trying to herd her scattered thoughts, Gage Hamilton, her best friend's husband and the owner of Last Frontier Lodge came skiing over to her side. He stopped and looked down, his gray eyes warm and concerned. "You okay? Saw you fall there."

Gage's question nudged her out of her trance, a thread of irritation rising. She hated having anyone concerned about her. "I'm fine," she said archly.

Gage's eyes crinkled with his smile. He glanced to the

man whose feet she'd landed by. "How's it going, Cam? Getting a feel for the trails yet?"

So the ski god had a name. Cam. Ginger wondered how Gage knew Cam.

Cam nodded. "It's going great. I've had a chance to ski every downhill trail so far. I was thinking of switching to my telemark skis and heading out on the backcountry trails this afternoon."

Gage grinned. "Perfect. We've got a good mix of trails out there. You'll find some easy cross country trails and a few challenging ones where you'll need those telemark skis." Gage glanced to Ginger. "I know you fell at Cam's feet, but did you get a chance to meet him?" Gage asked with a wink and a sly smile.

Her cheeks flamed again, but she managed to roll her eyes. Cam might fluster her, but she could handle Gage. "We haven't had much time to talk," she replied, biting back a huff.

Cam looked from Gage to her, meeting her eyes straight on. "Cam Nash," he said with a nod.

If Ginger didn't know better, she'd seriously think Cam had special powers. Whenever he looked directly at her with those warm amber eyes, her belly fluttered and a soft buzz of electricity swirled between them. She suddenly realized she was just standing there with Gage and Cam looking at her expectantly. Right, it was her turn to actually speak, something she usually had no trouble with. She was a speech therapist for crying out loud. An undergraduate degree and two graduate degrees had given her absolutely no training on what to do when a man robbed you of the capacity to speak by his mere presence. Once again, she gathered herself and called upon her manners.

"N-n-nice to meet you. I'm Ginger Sanders. Are you here for a visit?" She managed to sound only slightly flustered once she got past the first word.

Cam shrugged. "Not exactly. I took a job here for the winter."

Gage nodded enthusiastically. "Cam is a world class skier and backcountry guide. Can't believe we lucked out and signed him on for the season. He's getting our ski school up and running and will hopefully help me expand our backcountry trails."

Oh. Dear. God. Cam would be here all the time. She'd hoped this was a passing encounter with a sexy tourist who she might see once or twice more. But no, he'd be here all the time. Maybe this was just a weird thing from her fall. She'd be fine in a few minutes. She'd better be. She was at Last Frontier Lodge all the time. Gage's wife, Marley, was her best friend, and the lodge had become one of the hottest local spots in town since it reopened. She couldn't be mooning about over Cam. She wouldn't. With her pulse running wild and butterflies twirling in her belly, she managed to smile politely.

"That's great! You'll love it here."

A whole two sentences and she ran out of words. Under usual circumstances, she would've happily stood with Cam and Gage and chatted about Diamond Creek, how awesome it was to have Last Frontier Lodge up and running again, and so on and so forth. Instead, she glanced around quickly for her skis, only to find them held in Cam's hand. "I, uh, should get going."

She reached for her skis, promptly knocking one loose from Cam's grip. He caught it easily. "I can carry these back if you need," he offered.

"No thanks, I got it." Her words came out rapidly. She practically snatched the skis from his hands and ran up to the sprawling back deck of the lodge. She must have looked like an idiot running in her heavy ski boots, but she didn't give a damn. She was all kinds of rattled by Cam Nash and needed a few minutes to pull herself together.

She put her skis away in the small shed Gage set aside for friends and family and made her way into the lodge. She shook her jacket off and looped it over her arm as she walked into the kitchen. Her friend, Delia Hamilton, was in the middle of kneading dough. Delia was married to Gage's brother, Garrett, who'd fallen head over heels in love with her when he came to Alaska for a visit. Ginger caught her eyes. "Okay if I use your bathroom?"

Delia nodded. "Of course!"

Ginger walked into Delia's office. Delia managed the kitchen and reception staff for the ski lodge, so she had one of the few private spaces downstairs in the lodge. Ginger stepped into the small bathroom and closed the door behind her. Leaning her hands on the edge of the counter, she stared in the mirror. Her shiny brown hair was a wild mess. She carefully brushed her fingers through it in a vain attempt to straighten it out. She took a deep breath, turned on the faucet and splashed cold water on her face in the hopes she could ease the heat suffusing her. By the mere age of twenty-eight, she'd been married and divorced. Her divorce had been full of ugly secrets spilling out, mostly the long list of acquaintances her ex had screwed around with. She'd thought she was good and done with men after that. Cam Nash had gone and proved her wrong, and he didn't even know it.

She'd committed herself to a life of freedom from men. Oh, she believed in love and happily-ever-after. Just not for her. It had all been going swimmingly. Two years had passed since her divorce and not once had it occurred to her she might meet someone who challenged her resolve. She'd found it quite easy to avoid men. No one she encountered appealed to her in the slightest. It wasn't because there weren't attractive men around. She lived in Alaska, which was filled to the brim with rugged, sexy men. So many, they had a damn calendar for them. She figured she'd developed a convenient immunity. Until Cam. Even now, a full five minutes away from his presence, her skin was still flushed and her belly fluttered at the thought of his amber eyes.

CHAPTER 2

Cam watched Ginger Sanders run off, her brown hair swinging about her shoulders. He glanced back at Gage. "Well, I guess she was in a hurry."

Gage looked puzzled, but he shrugged. "Guess so. Ginger's a good friend. You'll see her around a lot. Aside from the fact she's Marley's best friend, she's probably our best source of local advertising around."

Cam was only just now getting a handle on himself. When Ginger had come skidding to a stop by his feet, he'd looked down into the most beautiful pair of blue eyes he'd ever seen—a bright, almost translucent shade of blue. Those eyes paired with her glossy brown hair and fair skin, she simply took his breath away. She had an understated quality to her beauty. There she sat, covered in snow, and he could hardly stop looking at her.

He shook his head, forcing his attention back to the moment. He'd best get used to seeing Ginger because it sounded like he'd be seeing a lot of her. If there was one thing he couldn't manage right now, it was anything to do with romance and women. He looked back at Gage.

"Well, no wonder you're so busy. Most lodges like this don't have so many locals. Not only is the hotel booked, but the slopes are twice as busy with the local skiers. If Ginger's responsible for your local advertising, she's damn good at it."

Gage threw his head back with a laugh. "I'll have to tell her you said that." He sobered and looked up the slope Cam had just skied down. "Did you find the trail leading off to the side up there?"

"Yup. It's behind the small cabin up there, right?"

Gage nodded. "That'll take you through the trees and onto the trails for back country and cross country skiing. So far, I've got about twenty miles of trails, but I'd like to double that. The trees are thin enough, so we don't need to do much cutting. We should be able to work around the natural lay of the land. Take a look and let me know what you think."

"That was my plan. I'll head up there now as soon as I switch out my skis."

At that, he and Gage pushed off on their skis simultaneously. He followed Gage up onto the back deck of the lodge. While Gage went inside, Cam quickly swapped his downhill skis for his more versatile telemark skis and headed back out. Telemark skis were designed for variation. They could handle downhill and cross-country and had enough flex to tolerate rougher trails if needed. As he rode up the lift, he realized the lodge could charge for the view from the lift ride alone. Diamond Creek, Alaska lay on the shores of Kachemak Bay with mountains rising tall behind it and on the far side of the bay. The ski lift offered an elevated view. The pristine waters of the bay sparkled under the early afternoon sunlight. The spruce forest scattered over the mountains was lush and deep green, the snow standing out in contrast.

Cam pushed off the ski lift when it reached its stop and

skied onto the start of an interconnected map of back-country trails. As he skied through the quiet forest, he breathed in the crisp mountain air. The air here held the subtlest hint of ocean. In all his years of skiing, he'd always skied in landlocked areas, so it was a new experience to be high in the mountains and see and smell the ocean. His mind was quietest when he skied, which is what brought him here to this remote corner of the world.

Skiing had been the center of his world for most of his life. He'd been born and raised in the mountains of Utah and skied throughout childhood, chasing his older brother, Eric. Two years older than Cam, Eric had been Cam's idol. They'd skied together and competed, taking turns winning. Their rivalry had been good-natured, though Eric took competition more seriously than Cam. One night, after Cam unexpectedly won a race, Eric had been sullen and silent on the drive home. When Cam asked him what was wrong, Eric glanced over right as a truck came around the corner on the icy road. In a split second, the car clipped the corner of the truck and skidded, colliding with the guardrail and bouncing over. Eric hadn't worn his seatbelt and was thrown from the car. He died on impact.

Cam, on the other hand, had worn his seat belt. He'd sustained some nasty bruises, a jagged cut on his cheek, and a fractured arm. Since the day he walked out of the hospital, he could hardly breathe for the grief at times. He'd tried to make a go of it in Utah, but it was filled with one too many painful memories. He couldn't stop skiing because it was the only thing that brought him a modicum of peace, so he'd been drifting from ski lodge to ski lodge, following the jobs. When he'd seen the ad for Last Frontier Lodge, he figured it was perfect. It was one of the few ski lodges he and Eric had never visited. They likely would have had it been opened during their heyday, but it had been shuttered for almost two decades until Gage reopened it.

Cam stopped along the trail at an overlook. A small valley opened up beside the trail with a stream winding through it. It was frozen in the deep of winter, but the sun struck sparks off the ice. A pair of moose stood on the far side of the field, lazily nibbling on a cluster of trees. He lifted his eyes up beyond the field. The bay spread out before him in the distance with another mountain range rising tall on the other side. If he didn't know there was a ski lodge nearby and a town at the foot of these mountains, he could convince himself he was in the middle of nowhere. He took a gulp of the bracing air and tried to push the pain of Eric's death out of his mind. In his effort to think of anything else, his mind flashed to Ginger. Simply picturing her chased thoughts of Eric out of his mind. He couldn't say why, but he couldn't forget her eyes, so bright and with a flicker of vulnerability that called to him.

* * *

A FEW HOURS LATER, Cam walked downstairs through the hall toward the lodge restaurant after a shower. He was good and tired from skiing almost all day and starving as a result. As he walked, he was staring at the floor, idly following the pattern of the carpet, when he collided with someone. He looked up, straight into Ginger's eyes. She wasn't wearing ski clothes that obscured her figure anymore. Oh no. She wore a pair of pants that hugged her full hips and swirled around her ankles, and a blouse that was fitted at the top and with a scoop neck. The curves of her full breasts rose above her blouse. As his eyes made their way up, he could see her pulse fluttering in her neck. *Oh damn. Damn.* One look, and she grabbed hold and sent lust surging through him.

He literally had to force his eyes up, only to have them land on her lips, which were plump and full. Her bright blue eyes held a sharp gleam. She had an edge to her he hadn't noticed before.

"Well, hello Cam. Fancy meeting you here. Are you heading in for dinner?"

Cam found himself nodding though he couldn't seem to speak.

"How about you join me and Marley?" she asked. "I figure since you're here for a while, we might as well be friends."

CHAPTER 3

Ginger slammed her car door behind her and hurried through the icy air into the post office. Today was one of those bitter cold days. For the most part, she enjoyed winter with its snowy landscape and the sheer beauty of the snow-capped mountains. Everything felt sharper, brighter and so fleeting with the abbreviated days of winter. Living in Alaska, it was a damn good thing to enjoy winter. But the days she didn't enjoy were like today. A cold, biting wind blew steadily. The sun, so precious in winter when every second of daylight counted, was hiding behind a wall of heavy gray clouds. No snow fell, so everything felt gray and frozen. She couldn't ever seem to get warm on days like this no matter how many layers she wrapped around herself. The warm blast of air that hit her when she pushed through the door into the post office was a heavenly relief.

The post office was a central place in Diamond Creek. In the far flung towns of Alaska, post offices were relied on much more heavily than in more urban areas. Many Alaskans conducted the majority of their shopping via mail.

Ginger glanced around, her eyes coasting across many familiar faces. She was so chilled, she wouldn't have minded if she needed to wait in the slow-moving line at the counter. She tugged her gloves off and loosened her scarf as she made her way to the aisle that held her post office box. It had been a few too many days since she'd checked her mail, so the box was stuffed. After yanking the pile of mostly junk mail out, she stationed herself at a table by the windows and made her way through the stack, tossing most of it in the recycling bin under the table.

She glanced out the window and saw Cam Nash walking across the parking lot. He was like a magnet for her eyes. The second he appeared, her eyes tracked him across the parking lot. He was distractingly handsome, which flustered her. She'd believed herself immune from any man. After she fell at his feet the other day, she'd determined she'd play it cool and move right past the silly attraction she felt. With him working at Last Frontier Lodge, she knew she needed to get a grip because she was going to end up seeing him a lot. With that in mind, when she'd seen him walking toward the restaurant, she'd called upon her usual bold self and invited him to eat dinner with her and Marley. She'd hoped the whole 'fake it 'til you make it' would hold her in good stead. She'd fake calm, cool, and collected around him and it would be so.

No such luck. With Cam sitting across from her and her best friend, she'd been distracted and flushed the entire time. Marley looked askance at her a few times, but there were enough interruptions from other friends and customers, Ginger had managed to avoid any questions from Marley and excused herself early. Now, she watched him shoulder through the door and pause to hold it for another person coming in behind him. The wind swirled through the door as it closed, sending the remainder of her mail in a spin with a few pieces of mail blowing on the floor. Relieved for the distraction from staring at Cam, since she could barely keep her eyes off of him, she bent over to collect the scattered mail.

A pair of boots came into sight. She glanced up to find Cam looking down at her. Her pulse immediately took off. She felt a literal pull inside—physical and emotional—and it unsettled her. She didn't like how easily he affected her. She gathered the last few envelopes and stood quickly.

His amber eyes crinkled at the corners when he smiled. "I thought that was you. Didn't mean to send your mail flying. It's pretty windy out there. How's it going?" he asked.

Trying and completely failing to slow her pulse, Ginger stared at Cam. His golden brown hair was windblown. He wore a pair of faded jeans topped with a cotton jersey shirt and heavy down jacket, which he'd left unzipped. Inconveniently, this made it possible for her eyes to trace the sculpted muscles of his chest and abdomen visible under his shirt. As her eyes, over which she'd lost all voluntary control, made their way up to his face, her belly somersaulted when she caught his warm amber gaze. *Now would be the time where you say hello. You remember how to do that, right? Oh shut up.* She snipped back at her critical voice and took a breath.

"It's going fine. Are you getting settled in at the lodge?"

Cam nodded. "Yeah, pretty much. Gage gave me a nice suite, so I've got everything I need. I haven't been here long, but honestly, it's one of the best places I've worked so far. Gage is great, and the lodge and trails are amazing. I'm finally venturing around town some. Diamond Creek is small, but it's got some high-end restaurants and shopping. It's also flat out beautiful. I love the mountains and the ocean, so being in a place where I get to enjoy both is unbelievable."

She felt a curl of pride. Born and raised in Diamond Creek, there had been times when she'd chafed at growing up in a tiny town on the wild coast of Alaska. A few years away in college and she'd learned Diamond Creek had a lot to offer, in addition to having a tight-knit, supportive community. Cam also put the conversation on a topic she could talk about easily, even with her pulse pounding wildly and heat sliding through her veins.

"Diamond Creek may be small, but we get a lot of tourists, so most of the restaurants and shops cater to them. It's hard to beat the views around here. Up at the lodge, you've got some of the best views around."

"Oh yeah. I was telling Gage he could charge for the lift rides if he wanted," Cam offered with a soft chuckle. "Haven't seen you skiing since the other day. Planning on coming up again soon?"

Ginger obviously couldn't tell him the sole reason she hadn't been skiing since last week when she fell at his feet was because he flustered her so much she couldn't think straight. She was usually up there several times a week skiing with Marley or other friends. She was about out of excuses, so she clung to the idea if she just kept ignoring this incredibly inconvenient attraction to Cam, it would go away. "It's been a busy week. I usually head up on the weekends though, so I'll probably be up there tomorrow."

The door pushed open again with another swirl of wind blowing through the entrance area. Marley Hamilton's auburn hair was impossible to miss when pushed her hood back and glanced around. As soon as her eyes landed on Ginger, a smile spread across her face. She strode to them and threw her arm over Ginger's shoulder. "Hey! I was just saying to Gage I hadn't seen you in a few days. How come you haven't been by?"

Ginger's cheeks got hot, but she forced herself to keep her expression calm. "I'll probably be up tomorrow. It's been a crazy week at work."

Marley nodded and turned to Cam. "Did you stop by Misty Mountain like I suggested?"

"Of course. Their coffee was as good as you promised," he replied with a smile.

Marley's green eyes bounced between them. "I told Cam he needs to get out and about. He's hardly left the lodge since he got here two weeks ago. I told him he needed to check out Misty Mountain Café, The Boathouse, Sally's, Glacier Pizza..."

Cam's eyes landed on Ginger again, and Marley's voice faded as she rattled off various local favorites. Ginger could have sworn he noticed she was about to melt. Between her pulse galloping beyond her control and the liquid heat building inside of her every time he looked her way, she was feeling ridiculous. Marley finally stopped talking and glanced between them. "Did you hear anything I just said?" she asked, directing her question to Ginger.

Ginger scrambled to pull her thoughts together and form words. "Of course I did! You were telling Cam all the places you said he should check out." She mentally breathed a sigh of relief when Marley nodded and turned to Cam again.

"So, Gage said you guys are going to get started on the back country trails. Any idea how many trails you think you can get cleared for grooming this season? Ginger and I used to go cross-country skiing all the time when we were kids, but now we have to drive clear across town to the local park if we want to go."

"I've scouted out the area and marked some trails already. He's ordered a tracksetter and..."

"What's a tracksetter?" Marley interjected.

"It's what will actually smooth down and groom the trails once we clear them. It's a contraption that hitches onto the back of a snowmobile. We'll ride along the trails with it to keep the snow packed and smooth. Depending on how many people start skiing on them, we'll see how often we need to use it. At least once or twice a week at a minimum."

Ginger couldn't believe it, but all she wanted to do was listen to Cam talk. His voice was warm with a gruff edge. It sent hot shivers coursing through her. *You are seriously out of your mind. You are so into this man you just want him to talk. What the hell is wrong with you? We had a deal. No more men. It's been easy peasy for a few years now. Cam is just new and exciting.* Ginger lost track of what Marley was saying and only heard the slow rumble of Cam's voice while the content of his words was entirely lost on her.

Marley nudged her shoulder. "Yoo hoo?"

Ginger whipped her eyes away from Cam and to Marley. "Huh?"

"Wow, you are seriously spaced out."

Ginger's cheeks heated again, and she forced herself to take a deep breath. She couldn't seem to be anywhere near Cam without embarrassing herself. "Right. Sorry. Just tired."

"I should get going anyway. I'll check my mail and be on my way," Cam said to both of them.

"I'm sure I'll see you back at the lodge," Marley said with a quick smile.

"I'm sure you will." His eyes canted to Ginger. "Hope to see you skiing again soon," he offered with a half-smile before he turned away.

Ginger fumbled for the stack of mail she'd set on the table. Someone else passed by and greeted Marley, which gave Ginger a few moments to gather her wits. She watched Cam reappear at the end of an aisle with his mail before he pushed through the door outside. The icy blast of air that swirled around soothed the heat coursing through her.

Marley leaned her elbow on the table and looked at Ginger. "Okay, what's up with you?" she asked.

Marley was Ginger's oldest friend. They'd grown up

together in Diamond Creek and been there for each other through everything. Even when Marley moved away to Seattle, their friendship stayed tight. When Ginger's marriage fell apart, Marley had called her every day for weeks and had flown up from Seattle to stay with her for a bit. When Marley's life skidded sideways after she was robbed in Seattle, Ginger had been the first person she called. Ginger couldn't imagine life without Marley and loved her as family. The one and only downside to having a friend as close and supportive as Marley was she was damn perceptive.

Ginger was relieved Cam had left because her body was behaving normally again. Her pulse had finally slowed, and the fluttery feeling inside was subsiding. She took a breath. "What do you mean?" She tried to hedge, hoping Marley would leave it alone.

Marley's green eyes narrowed. "Uh, let's see. You hardly spoke the whole time Cam was standing here, and you kept staring at him. If I had to guess, I'd say you might have a thing for him." A grin spread slowly across Marley's face.

Ginger felt her cheeks heat again. She put her face in her hands and sighed. "I do *not* have a thing for him, but he might be kind of cute." She dropped her hands and fiddled with the mail, riffling through the envelopes and tossing a few more pieces of junk mail in the recycling bin. She glanced up at Marley again who was still grinning.

"He's a lot more than cute. You should hear the girls in housekeeping and the restaurant babbling about him." As Marley looked over at Ginger, her grin faded. "Hey, I'm just teasing. It's okay to notice a man, you know."

Ginger's chest tightened, a wash of vulnerability followed by anger knotting inside. She hated feeling vulnerable like this, at the mercy of the whims of desire. She prided herself on being in control and together. A few minutes in Cam's presence revealed the fault lines in her resolve. "I know, but it's not worth it."

Marley was quiet for a long moment. "Okay, we're grabbing dinner at Sally's. Give me a sec." She whirled away and jogged down another aisle, returning quickly with a handful of mail. She looped her hand through Ginger's elbow. "Come on. You don't get to say no. We haven't had dinner, just you and me, in weeks."

Ginger didn't hesitate. She didn't want to talk about Cam, but she could use some advice. Because really, it wasn't Cam. It was all the baggage she was carting around that had everything to do with men and romance. She'd braved her way through her divorce and somehow cobbled together her pride after it was over. So much of her pride relied on her confidence that she wouldn't let herself be vulnerable again. Her attraction to Cam, so powerful and so fast, was testing her confidence. The fear she'd walled inside her heart was seeping out because those walls weren't as strong as she'd believed.

Marley tugged Ginger through the icy wind and into her car. Moments later, they were walking through the door in Sally's. Sally's was a fixture in Diamond Creek. It was a restaurant and bar housed in an old refurbished barn. The kitchen was in the center with one side holding the bar with a stage for music and performances. The other side held the restaurant with tables filling the center and booths lining the walls. The old hayloft held additional seating that wrapped around the upstairs. Ginger and Marley had spent so much time here over the years, a sense of comfort washed over her simply walking inside.

They snagged the only available booth. After a waitress took their order, Marley leaned back and eyed Ginger. "Are you okay?" she asked softly.

Ginger busied herself unrolling the napkin around the silverware. She looked across the table at Marley and took a breath. "I'm fine. As you noticed, I, uh, kind of noticed Cam is, well, Cam." She couldn't help the laugh that bubbled up.

Marley's laugh rang out with hers. "Cam is most definitely Cam. He might not do much for me, but I'm not blind."

Ginger rolled her eyes. "It's amazing you see anyone other than Gage. It's been over a year and you two are still like new lovebirds."

This time, Marley flushed. "Maybe so. Don't forget you practically pushed me into his arms."

Ginger shrugged. "Maybe I did. It was obvious you two were meant for each other."

Marley nodded as her eyes sobered. "So back to Cam."

"Right. Since you already noticed, I might think he's pretty hot. Problem is, that's not supposed to happen."

Marley's brows hitched up, her eyes puzzled. Their waitress arrived and quickly placed a beer for Ginger and water for Marley on the table before she turned away to serve the next booth. Ginger took a swallow from her beer and leaned back with a sigh. Marley followed her movements minus the sigh. "Gotta say, I cannot wait to be able to have alcohol again," she said as she rubbed her round belly. Marley and Gage were expecting a little girl due in roughly a month.

"Not much longer. How're you feeling? You hardly ever complain."

"Honestly, it's been pretty okay until a few weeks after Christmas. Since then, I just feel gigantic." She shook her head and shrugged. "Anyway, back to you. What do you mean it's not supposed to happen?"

Ginger took another gulp from her beer and mentally pushed back against the old feeling of vulnerability. She thought she was past this. Her grand plan to never be attracted to another man had been working out great. She'd convinced herself she was immune, and then Cam had to come along and blow her confidence out of the water.

"After everything went down with Tony, I decided it would be best if I just didn't get involved with anyone ever again. It's not worth it, not for me. It's been a piece of cake. I mean, Alaska is overrun with men. Maybe half of them are a little too rough for wear, but there are plenty of hot guys around between the outdoorsy types, the skiers, the hunters and what-not. Not a single man has even made me think about sex, so I thought it would be easy."

Marley leaned forward, shaking her head. "Wait, you're saying you seriously thought you'd go through the rest of your life and never be attracted to anyone? Ever?"

Ginger flushed. Hearing Marley say it aloud made it sound ridiculous. Yet, Ginger had thought it reasonable, especially since it seemed to be working. She'd decided she wouldn't bother with relationships and since no one, absolutely no one, drew the slightest bit of response from her, she figured she had it made. She wouldn't need to worry about falling for the wrong guy and looking like a fool later.

"Yes. I seriously thought it just wouldn't happen. I know it sounds crazy..."

Marley nodded vigorously.

"Maybe it was crazy, but I don't want to go through what I went through with Tony. It sucked. You have no idea how stupid I felt."

Marley nodded. "I know it was awful. Noticing Cam doesn't have to be anything more than that, you know."

Ginger shrugged. "I know. It just brings up all kinds of crap that I didn't want to ever deal with again."

Their waitress arrived with their meals. Ginger nibbled on a few fries, while Marley took a bite of her burger. A few moments later, Marley looked over again. "Okay, how about you take a step back? Cam is damn easy on the eyes, and you and probably every woman who meets him notices that. There's no need to get all worked up."

Ginger took a bite of her burger, considering Marley's words as she chewed. She liked thinking about Cam that way. So she thought he was hot? She was probably just freaking out over nothing. She nodded. "Right. That's all it is. I'm just half-whacked when it comes to men."

Marley shook her head. "No you're not. Tony was a total ass to you. I'd have felt like a fool if I were you. Not that you should have, but that's how it goes. Trust me, everyone looking in from the outside saw it for exactly what it was. Tony treated an amazing woman like shit," Marley said emphatically. She paused for a sip of water. "You're not freaking out over Cam, you're freaking out over what he represents. Face it, it was silly to think you'd never be attracted to anyone again. Maybe it's good Cam came along. You'll realize it's not the end of the world." Her eyes softened and she set her burger down. "How about next time you come up with a half-baked plan like that you tell me about it sooner, so I can point out how ridiculous it is?"

Ginger finished the last bite of her burger and sighed. "Because saying it out loud made it seem insane."

Marley chuckled. "Plus, you're all over making sure the rest of us find our soul mates."

Ginger grinned. "I believe in love. I just figured I'd already had my shot."

Marley rolled her eyes. "Look, I might be biased because you're my best friend, but you're smart, amazing and gorgeous. Even if you're not looking, someone will find you. Maybe it won't be Cam, maybe it will be, but you can sure enjoy looking at him in the meantime."

Ginger balled up her napkin and tossed it at Marley.

CHAPTER 4

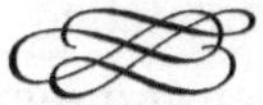

A snowball flew through the air and landed with a thump in the center of Cam's chest. A gust of wind blew the exploding ball of snow into his face. He brushed the snow out of his eyes and glanced around. A little boy stood across from him with his mouth hanging open and his cheeks beet red.

"It was him!" Another boy declared, pointing to the boy Cam had just noticed.

"No! It was you!" This declaration came from another boy who promptly punctuated his accusation with a snowball that careened off course in the wind and blew sideways.

In seconds, several more boys joined in and snowballs were flying wildly in the cluster. Cam leaned on one of his ski poles and chuckled. Today was the first day of a ski class he started for children aged eight to ten. He'd started skiing when he was even younger, so he was a big proponent of starting young. Skiing was a great way to burn off restless energy and taught concentration and coordination. Plus, it was damn fun. With Gage's agreement, he was running weekly courses for visitors to the lodge, in addition to classes that ran throughout winter for locals. Today's class was for the locals. Another snowball bounced off his shoulder, at which point, he blew the whistle he kept on him solely for this purpose. At the sound of the piercing whistle, the cluster of boys stopped throwing snow and turned in unison to stare at him. His eyes traveled over the motley bunch. A few boys were suited up in good gear, while others were bundled up in mismatched outfits. All were clearly accustomed to the weather and seemed entirely unbothered by the temperature, which hadn't quite hit ten degrees Fahrenheit yet.

He put his hands on his hips. "Okay boys, only five minutes a day for snowball fights. You're out of time, so let's get started. Does everyone have their skis?"

In seconds, the snow covered boys were shuffling around and gathering up their skis and poles. The next two hours passed quickly. Cam had initially balked at teaching skiing back when he first started picking up jobs at ski lodges years ago when he and Eric traveled around together. Then, he discovered he enjoyed it. With a few exceptions, most children who showed up wanted to learn to ski. His passion for it made it easy to teach. He wouldn't have called himself a patient man before he started teaching, but he found a patience he hadn't known he had. He could see it would be much harder to corral the wild energy of some of the kids if it weren't for the fact skiing was an active sport that kept their minds and bodies occupied. Today's group was comprised of boys who had all skied at some point. They were here to learn finesse and improve their skills. Cam helped each of them gather up their skis and followed them to the sprawling deck at the back of the lodge where their parents were waiting.

After he watched the last boy trundle across the deck, a loose ski dragging behind him, he leaned against the railing and looked out toward the mountains rising behind the lodge. It was early afternoon and the slopes were dotted with skiers. The bright colors of their jackets stood out against the snow.

"How'd the lesson go?"

Cam turned to find Gage approaching him. "Pretty good. Aside from a few snowball fights, they worked hard. Any word yet on when that tracksetter will get here?"

Gage leaned against the railing beside him. "Don figures it'll get here later this week. Once we get the first run done, we can turn this over to Don. He loves working outside, and this looks like it won't be too hard on him."

Don Peters was Gage's right-hand man at the lodge. Cam had quickly discovered Don knew the ins and outs of running a ski lodge better than most. He'd managed the slopes and grounds for the lodge in its earlier era for over twenty years. Cam enjoyed working alongside him, mostly because Don clearly loved Last Frontier Lodge and was beside himself when Gage reopened it after so many years. Gage had carefully taken Cam aside and asked him to be sensitive about the fact Don wasn't as young as he once was.

Cam caught Gage's eyes and nodded. "He'll enjoy handling the trail grooming. Once we've marked the trails and gotten them leveled the first time, it's mellow work. It's basically a snowmobile ride. The tracksetter hitches to the back and does the work for you."

"Sounds good. How about you and I head up there tomorrow and keep marking more trail?"

"Tell me what time to meet you, and we can head up together."

Gage shrugged. "Let's see how the morning goes and maybe plan for late morning. You want to meet for an early dinner in the restaurant in a bit?" At Cam's nod, Gage continued. "Does five work?"

"Yup. I was about to head in for a shower. Need me to take care of anything else right now?"

"Nope. We're covered on the slopes for the afternoon." Gage's cell phone buzzed. He slipped the phone out of his pocket and glanced at the screen. "I need to take this," he commented before stepped away and answering as he walked across the deck.

Cam turned back to the mountains and breathed in the cold air. An eagle screeched in the distance followed by the call of a crow. He took a last look at the mountains before turning away and walking inside. He made his way to his hotel suite. The room was disconcertingly quiet. So many years of traveling to ski lodges had been spent with Eric. Even though they were in far flung locations, most ski lodges had a familiar feel to them. Last Frontier Lodge had the same familiar feeling—a feeling he savored because it meant he was where he wanted to be doing what he loved. Last Frontier Lodge ranked as one of the nicer lodges Cam had encountered. Gage had done a good job updating the place and had been generous in providing Cam with his own full suite. Yet, Eric's absence was a haunting echo. Sometimes Cam wondered if he should just walk away from skiing, but every time he considered it, he could hardly bear it. Skiing was too central to his life. He only wished it wasn't so tied to his late brother. He clung to the glimmer of hope that came from the pain starting to dull over time.

After he showered, he sat at the table by the windows and watched the sun slide down behind the mountains. The horizon was streaked with lavender and pink, the cool colors of winter sunsets. His phone sat on the table. His eyes kept bouncing to it and away. He finally reached over and slid the phone in front of him. He quickly tapped the screen, pulling up his mother's number. After several rings, she answered.

"Hey Cam! How's Alaska?"

"Hey Mom. Alaska's gorgeous. How are things there?"

"Just fine. We're both busy with work. We've had plenty

of snow here. I'm hoping the skiing is as good there as it is here this winter because if not, you might want to get back here."

He smiled. His mom knew how much he loved skiing. She'd be worried he'd miss the good snow. "No need to worry, Mom. We've got plenty of snow here in Diamond Creek. You and Dad should come up if you can. You'd love it."

"We probably will. I was just telling your father maybe we could get up there later this winter. So, how are you?"

Cam could imagine her expression. Her brown eyes would be warm and concerned. He could feel her soft smile through the phone. Eric's death, of course, had been a blow for her and his father. Yet, Cam felt so alone in his grief. It didn't matter how many times he tried to tell himself he couldn't blame himself, he did. If he hadn't said anything at that moment, Eric wouldn't have looked over and he wouldn't have clipped the truck and the car accident wouldn't have happened. Cam felt tears press at the back of his eyes. He took a deep breath and looked out over the mountains into the swirl of colors. Stars were dotting the sky through the fading light. Another breath, and he thought he could manage answering.

"I'm okay, Mom. I'm glad I found this place. It's beautiful. The owner is a great guy to work for, and it's giving me time to get my feet back under me. How are you?"

"Oh, you know. We're doing okay. I stay busy at the library, and your dad's store is having its best year yet. We just want to know you're okay. Promise me you'll let me know if you need anything."

"I will, Mom. How about you check with Dad and let me know when you think you two can come up for a visit?"

"You got it. I'll talk to him tonight."

"Okay. I gotta go, but I'll call again this weekend. Love you, Mom."

"Love you."

Her warm words pinged in his heart, still sore every time he thought about Eric. He leaned back in his chair and sighed. He had another call to make, so he tapped his screen again, this time pulling up his sister's number. Her voice mail picked up. *"Hey, it's Ivy. You know what to do."*

"Hey Ivy, give me a call when you can. Miss you," he said to her voice mail.

He set the phone back down, a smile curving his lips. Just thinking about Ivy made him smile. Ivy was ten years younger than him and kept him on his toes. She was the brilliant one in the family and was currently finishing up a graduate degree in mechanical engineering. After Eric died, she'd taken a semester off and prodded Cam through the darkest months after Eric's death.

He glanced at the clock above the door and stood from the table. Moments later, he made his way down the hallway toward the lodge restaurant. He fumbled around in his pocket to make sure he had his keys. He suddenly remembered he'd left them in his truck. When he reached the reception area, he veered through the main entrance and out to the parking lot. After he reached his truck and snagged his keys from above the visor, he started to walk back to the lodge when he noticed a car stopped at the head of the long driveway. He waited to see if the vehicle was about to move when he saw a form silhouetted in the headlights leaning over the check one of the front tires.

"DAMMIT!" Ginger pounded on the steering wheel.

She'd just turned into the drive at Last Frontier Lodge when she noticed her tire felt squishy. She hadn't had too may flat tires in her life, but the feeling was distinct. She stopped where she was and climbed out. A quick check and she confirmed her suspicion. The last thing she wanted to deal with was changing her tire in the cold darkness. "Dammit!" she said again to no one.

Or so she thought. "Dammit, what?" a voice replied.

She swung around and saw a tall, lanky form approaching her down the lodge drive. The lights from the lodge didn't quite reach this far, but they offered a soft halo of thin light. As the form got closer, she saw it was Cam. Her body instantly tightened and her pulse quickened. She didn't know what to do with how she reacted to him. All he had to do was show up and electricity buzzed through her, rattling her to her core.

"Flat tire," she called out softly.

Cam came to a stop at her side and glanced down. He arched a brow. "Ah. Well, I suppose it's a good thing you made it to the drive."

She stood up and brushed her hands off. "I suppose. I still have to get it changed out though, so I might as well take care of it now."

What she left unsaid was the fact she desperately needed something to do. Changing a tire would keep her occupied. *Remember what Marley said. He's just a man. You happen to think he's hot, but so do plenty of women. It's nothing more than a little appreciation. Oh, now come on. This is waaaay more than a little appreciation.*

Ginger swatted the voice away and walked rapidly to the back of her car. She popped the hatch open and started to tug the spare tire out. She half hoped Cam would just walk away. He didn't. He came to the back of her car, lifted the tire from her hands and got right to work. It was bad enough she was stumbling through her silly attraction to him, but he had to go and be even more irresistible by being helpful and annoyingly manly in his efficiency at changing her tire. She was so befuddled by his presence that she let him just take over, which wasn't usually how she was, but she didn't really care at the moment. Not much later, he stood up and glanced over at her.

"There you go. Your spare's in good shape, but you'll want to take it in and swap the spare out as soon as you can."

She nodded wordlessly. It was driving her nuts, but somehow Cam robbed her of the capacity to speak. And she liked to talk, damn it all. He stood in front of her, the jack resting in his hands. After a moment, he walked to the back of her car and put the jack and other tools away in the compartment on the side and closed the hatch.

When he turned to her, the air felt alive. Her breath caught in her throat, and her pulse hammered wildly. She was frozen in place. When she met his eyes in the darkness, they were locked on her. For this moment, she forgot everything—her uncertainties, her silly promise to never be attracted to a man again, and all the baggage she'd carted around for the last few years. Right now, all she wanted was a taste of Cam. He stood before her in the darkness, the lights from the lodge offering just enough light she could see the golden amber of his eyes. The air around them heated. Her low belly clenched and need rose within.

She stepped closer to him. For a second, she wondered if he'd step away, but he didn't. She lifted a hand and stroked it up his arm. He hadn't worn a jacket, so she could feel the shape of his muscles under her palm as she slid her hand up. She kept moving, her palm coasting across his sculpted chest and curling around his neck. A tiny corner of her mind wondered if she'd gone completely mad. Not only was she ignoring her promise to never be attracted to a man again, but she was about to kiss Cam.

Cam had been standing stock still, but he suddenly moved. He stepped closer to her, his amber eyes nearly burning into her. He opened his mouth as if to speak. Her heart was pounding so hard, she thought for certain he could hear it. "What are we doing?" he asked, his words rough.

"I want to kiss you." Her words were raw and bare. She was so out of her element, she couldn't even call upon her defenses to make her sensible again. All she wanted was this kiss. Right here, right now.

She felt his shoulders rise and fall with a deep breath before he nodded. "I suppose it's a good thing I want to kiss you too."

At his words, a flash of heat scored through her center. Ginger bit back a gasp at her body's swift reaction. She didn't wait and tugged him down to meet her as she leaned up. Cam's lips met hers. For a flicker, she hesitated. She hadn't kissed a man in over two years, so the feel of his lips against hers was unfamiliar. She pushed back against the feeling and threw herself into the kiss. If she was going to be stupid, she might as well make it worth her while. Problem was, she entirely underestimated how a kiss with Cam would feel. As soon as their lips touched, it was like a match to a flame. She gasped, and his tongue swept inside.

His arms slipped around her, his embrace strong and sure. She flexed into him, desperate to get closer. His kiss was everything she could have hoped for and more. She'd been so busy batting her fantasies away, she hadn't even allowed herself to imagine this kiss. He kissed masterfully. His tongue stroked against hers in between tracing her lips, he tugged at her bottom lip and dove in deep again. Liquid need swirled in her center. She was so wet, she could feel the moisture seeping through her underwear.

Cam's hand stroked up her back and laced into her hair, his touch hot and strong. He tore his lips from hers and lifted his head. Their breath gusted in the icy air. When he glanced back down, all she could do was stare at him. Desire thrummed through her body. She was caught in its sway.

She didn't want this to stop. Their eyes held, an electric current vibrating between them.

He swore softly, right before his lips crushed against hers again. She didn't quite know how it was possible, but this kiss eclipsed the first and went wild. It was a tangle of lips and tongues—hot, wet and deep. Out of breath and nearly overcome, when his lips made their way down her neck, hot shivers raced through her. She trembled against the onslaught on sensations. When his lips reached her collarbone, he dipped his forehead to rest in the curve of her shoulder. They held still in the cold darkness. The heat within and around them was so intense, she barely noticed it was near zero outside.

Cam's palm stroked in slow passes along her spine, sending tingles spiraling through her entire body. Her breathing gradually slowed, though her body felt alight from the desire pounding through her. The cold finally permeated her, and she shivered. He lifted his head. "We should get inside. It's freezing out here." His eyes locked onto hers, banked heat simmering in their amber depths.

She managed a nod, realizing she couldn't just stand out here all night in Cam's arms, although that was precisely what she'd have liked to do. Rational thought managed to nudge her though. At any moment, the slew of locals arriving for dinner at the lodge would start showing up. It was pure luck no one had driven by them yet. She took a breath. "Okay. Let me drive my car the rest of the way into the parking lot. Do you want to ride with me?"

It wasn't much of a distance, but she wasn't ready to let go of this tenuous and electric connection with him. At his nod, she got into her car and he walked around and climbed in the passenger side. In silence, she drove the short distance to the lodge parking lot. Moments later when they stood in front of the lodge entrance, Ginger looked up at Cam and her breath caught in her throat. He was so damn handsome. His amber hair was gold-tipped in the soft light under the entrance. His eyes coasted over her, and it was as if he touched her everywhere he looked. Heat slid through her again, and her pulse skittered wildly. She thought she should say something, but she didn't know what.

He saved her when he cleared his throat and spoke. "I, uh, didn't mean to let things get out of hand like that."

His words unintentionally struck at the doubts she'd carried deep in her heart for the last few years. Vulnerability and uncertainty lashed at her. She shook her head, somehow dredging up the brash side of herself. "Let's just call it one hell of a kiss. Okay?"

His mouth hooked up on one side and he nodded.

CHAPTER 5

Cam maneuvered his skis along a rough trail, carefully dodging a branch that had fallen across the trail. The sun was high in the sky. The snow glittered where it melted under the heat of the sun. He was leading Gage through the backcountry trails he'd marked thus far. He came to a stop beside a rough bridge he'd built to cross over a narrow stream. Gage skied to his side.

"You've made it farther than I guessed. You've added probably twenty more miles to what we already had," Gage said with a grin.

Cam tugged his gloves off and unzipped the top of his jacket. He'd worked up a sweat on the way out. Cool air sifted through the opening in his jacket. He glanced to the stream and back to Gage. "It wasn't too hard. Like you said, we didn't need to do much clearing. There are some rough areas though. I figure we settle on the layout for the trails and get everything marked, and then we can deal with getting rocks, roots and debris out of the way. After that, we use the tracksetter and we can open the course up for skiers."

"I've already said it, but I'll say it again. I'm damn glad I hired you. Until I got back up here year before last, I'd never cross-country skied in my life. All I'd ever done was downhill skiing and snowboarding. I didn't have a clue about what we needed to do for trails. Don knows the slopes and lifts backwards and forwards, but this part wasn't his gig either. Thanks to you, we'll be able to add this course for customers and locals. I keep going back and forth if I should charge for locals for this. There's a series of trails on the other side of town, but they're funded by the town park fund."

"You could charge a season fee like you do for the slopes," Cam suggested.

Gage idly twirled his ski pole and nodded. "Makes the most sense. So how much further do you think we should go with the trails?"

"Well, first you have to consider how much land you have for trails. Beyond that, you need to consider how accessible the area is if you need to get up here. Between what you had before and what I've roughed out, we've got about forty miles of trail now. That's more than enough. I followed your lead and made sure to loop the trails into each other, so you can access all of them within fifteen minutes by snowmobile if you need to. If you're asking my opinion..."

Gage interjected. "I definitely am."

"I'd stick with what we have now. Much more and it's a lot more maintenance and then you have to worry about accessibility."

Gage nodded firmly. "Okay then. We'll stop with what we have. We'll come back up tomorrow with the snowmobile and get to work on dealing with the debris."

"Sounds like a plan." Cam pulled his gloves back on. "You headed back down now?"

"Yeah. I promised Marley I wouldn't be gone too long. She's due any day now," Gage replied with a proud smile.

Cam was still amazed at how easily Marley was getting around. If it hadn't been so obvious she was pregnant, Cam would never have guessed. She stayed busy and was around and about the lodge every day. She wasn't skiing, but that seemed to be the only limit she'd given herself. "Well, you'd best get back down there then."

Gage turned on his skis and adjusted his hold on his ski poles. "Speaking of that, I guess we haven't really talked about me taking some time off after she has the baby. I don't really have a plan. I figure I'll play it by ear. Since I work right here, I'll be around no matter what."

"Well, you might as well take all the time you want. Don and I can take care of everything outside."

Gage grinned. "I know. Another reason I'm glad you're here." He lifted a ski pole and pushed off. "Meet me and Marley for dinner if you want," he said with a wave as he skied away.

Cam watched him go while he waited behind in the snowy forest. After the sound of Gage's skis faded, the only sound was the breeze blowing through the trees. Cam took a slow breath of air, savoring the hint of spruce and the subtle scent of the ocean in the distance. He pushed off on his skis and set out on a small loop he'd marked the other day. The rhythmic sound of his skis swishing across the snow settled him. Skiing was both painful and soothing these days. Too much of his time had been spent skiing with Eric, which meant now he had to adjust to Eric's absence. Years past, Eric would have been at his side on these trails. It was gradual, but the sharpness of the pain was dulling. He turned onto a long straight stretch and picked up his pace, pushing himself to go fast and hard over the snow. When he reached the end of the straight stretch, the trail dipped and curved down a hill. He flew over it, his skis flexing with his landing as he cut down the swerve and swirled to a stop at the bottom of the short hill. He'd pushed himself hard enough to savor the breath heaving in and out of his lungs. When he pushed himself physically, he forgot everything and only focused on the moment in time.

He held still at the bottom of the hill and looked out over the small field beside him. Snow blanketed everything. An eagle screeched loudly and flew out of the trees. His eyes tracked the majestic bird as it angled sideways, its wings casting a wide shadow on the snow below. As it flew above the trees, he looked past it to the mountain peaks on the far side of the bay. So regal and immense, they stood quietly, their shadows cast across the water. With a last look, he pushed off his skis and headed back to the lodge.

As he skied back, Ginger sauntered through his thoughts, which she'd been doing fairly frequently since their kiss last night. He had absolutely no idea what he'd been thinking. But once his lips touched hers, thought wasn't an option. Somehow, he'd fumbled his way through dinner afterwards. She'd set him afire and sent his heart into a tailspin, unsettling him in a way he hadn't expected. He was generally pretty quiet, so no one seemed to notice he had a hard time talking around her after that. She'd joined him with Gage and Marley for dinner. Don had spent a while with them, along with a few other friends and family. Cam had been at so many ski lodges, many of them were interchangeable. Last Frontier Lodge stood out for the sheer beauty of its location and its warm, friendly vibe. Gage and Marley had a standing dinner in the restaurant with any variety of family and friends joining them on different evenings. They'd easily welcomed Cam into their circle and went out of their way to make sure he felt comfortable.

He didn't want to mess up his welcome by stumbling over whatever this thing was with him and Ginger. All he'd known last night was he wanted to kiss her so badly he could hardly see straight. He'd like to think he had more control over himself. He could barely remember the last time he even noticed a woman. Before Eric died, his life was traveling and skiing. They bounced from race to race and were leaders in backcountry skiing all over the world. He had flings here and there, but he was so focused on staying in peak condition, even those weren't much of a part of his life. He hadn't thought about it much, but he always figured he'd find someone when his life slowed down. His parents had a good marriage, and he hoped to have the same someday. Then, Eric died and his life skidded sideways. Romance, casual or otherwise, hadn't even crossed his mind.

Until he laid eyes on Ginger. At first, he'd figured it was just an attraction and would fade. Yet, every time he saw her, the air snapped and crackled between them. Then, he'd gone and kissed her and all but lost his mind.

GINGER WAITED while Charlie Harris sounded out his words. She worked with Charlie twice a week. As a speech therapist, she dealt with a wide range of challenges with children. Charlie struggled with phonation and pitch, so his words were often difficult to understand. Charlie was a joy to work with because he was diligent and he tried so hard. As many children with communication difficulties did, he'd initially been referred to her after a few meltdowns in his pre-school class. She'd quickly deduced he was getting frustrated because no one understood what he was trying to communicate. At younger ages, speech problems weren't as obvious at first because children learned at different speeds. She was always pleased when a child landed with her early because her chances for progress were much greater.

Charlie's brown hair gleamed under the bright lights in her small classroom. His index finger moved to the last word on the list. After he successfully sounded it out, he looked up with an expectant smile.

"Great job, Charlie!" she said with a quick clap of her hands. "You did so well, you don't have to go through them again."

Charlie lifted his hand for a high five, a habit they'd developed during her time with him. "Am I all done today?"

"All done!" She glanced at the clock. "You've got a few minutes before the bell. Want to play a game of Uno?"

"Yeah!"

Charlie stood up and raced over to the cabinet where she kept an assortment of games. He knew precisely where Uno was because it was his favorite game. He was back at the table in seconds. She waited while he carefully dealt the cards. One area where Charlie didn't lack any skill was in pragmatic communication, or rather social communication. His words might not always be clear, but he was outgoing and friendly with just about anyone. He chattered on about his friends, his dog, and his favorite teacher.

When the bell rang, he carefully stacked the cards and handed them to her. "I'll see you next week, Ms. Sanders."

"You sure will. Bye, Charlie!" she called out when he reached the door.

He waved and was gone in a flash. She stepped to the door and closed it. Elementary schools were pure cacophony when children were switching classes. She could hardly hear herself think, so she usually kept her door closed. She sat down at her desk with a sigh. She quickly checked her email and took care of her notes from the morning students. Only then did her mind wander to Cam.

Her brain had taken a backseat to desire when she was standing beside him last night. She chuckled to herself. So often she had wished for an off switch for her mind to silence the internal chatter. She hadn't meant for her brain to turn off altogether so she did something crazy like tell Cam she wanted to kiss him and then go and do it. *What the hell were you thinking? Well, that's the problem. You weren't thinking. Maybe not, but that kiss was worth every second.* "Oh my God," she said aloud to herself. She flushed straight through just thinking about that kiss. It was the kiss to beat all kisses. She'd tried to convince herself last night, after the madness of the moment, that it would get Cam out of her system. But she knew damn well she was kidding herself. Every spare minute when she wasn't focused on something, her mind and body went right to Cam. He was like a magnet. Her hope that he'd be a brief infatuation was fading. Though his presence in her orbit was still fairly new, she wasn't dumb. She knew the attraction she felt for him was more than just passing.

She put her face in her hands and groaned. Somehow, she needed to wrest control of herself again. She ran her hands through her hair and sat back in her chair. While her mind could run wild thinking about Cam, she was short on ideas about how to get a handle on herself.

Later that afternoon, she resisted the urge to drive up to the lodge for dinner and drove home instead. She lived in a small house on a bluff by Kachemak Bay. The house was a simple cedar house. The downstairs was comprised of a living room with a kitchen to the side through an archway, and a small bathroom and laundry room to the other side. A wall of windows afforded a clear view of the rocky beach and bay. A dove gray soapstone woodstove sat in the center of the living room. A circular staircase led upstairs where there was one large bedroom suite with a bathroom and seating area by the windows. There were decks on both floors. She'd bought the home with what little money she walked away with after her divorce.

She walked inside and tossed her keys on the table by

the door. After she hung up her jacket and kicked off her shoes in the small closet by the door, she made her way into the kitchen. At that moment, her pet rabbit, George, bounded down the stairs. George was a gray lop-eared rabbit she'd adopted after her divorce. She adored him. He was house trained like a cat and bounded about freely. He often spent time on the decks and in the yard in the summer, but he eschewed going outside in the winter even when she tried to encourage him. He leapt onto a chair by the table and nudged her hand.

"Hey George. How was your day?" She sat down and set him on her lap. They sat that way for a few minutes while she petted him. When her stomach growled, she finally stood and stared into the refrigerator. In need of comfort food, she made a grilled cheese sandwich and ensconced herself on the couch with George to watch television. As she lay in bed later, Cam wove through her thoughts and she wondered just what the hell she'd gotten herself into. A part of her wished she'd seen him again today, so she could have tried to gauge how he felt. Yet, she was so muddled inside and so fraught with her own confusion and insecurity, she doubted she could accurately interpret anything when it came to Cam.

CHAPTER 6

"Scoot over," Marley said, waving her hand at Garrett Hamilton. "Make room for Cam."

Garrett flashed a grin. "Yes, ma'am," he replied as he slid across the seat in the booth.

Garrett Hamilton was Gage's brother and Delia's husband. From what Cam understood, Garrett used to be a workaholic lawyer in Seattle. His life now was a far cry from that, but he seemed entirely content. As far as Cam could tell, he was head over heels in love with Delia. Garrett shared his brother's dark hair paired with blue eyes. He turned his grin to Cam. "How's it going, Cam?"

"Pretty good. Keeping busy."

Garrett nodded. "Good thing you're here. Any day now, Marley'll have her baby, and Gage'll need you to pick up his slack." His eyes canted to Marley.

Marley smiled and leaned back in the booth. "You know Gage won't slack too much. He keeps saying he's going to take time off, but I won't be surprised if he manages only a week."

Garrett chuckled. "Probably."

Over the next little while, Cam enjoyed the banter with Marley, Gage and the rotating collection of family and friends who joined them for various amounts of time as dinner moved along. He found himself looking to the entrance over and over and realized he kept wondering if Ginger would show up. She wasn't here every evening, but was definitely here several times a week. He hadn't seen her since the night they'd kissed. Though it had only been a few days, a small corner of his mind worried she was avoiding him. It stung a little to think she might be.

"Where is Ginger anyway?" someone asked.

Cam turned in the direction of the question and saw it was Delia who'd asked. Delia was a lovely counterpoint to Garrett. He was tall and dark with an edge to his features and personality. Her honey gold hair and warm blue eyes fit with her friendly and kind nature. She tended to mother just about anyone who crossed her path. Whenever she was near, Garrett's energy softened. Cam had also discovered she was an absolutely amazing cook. She ran the lodge restaurant and was prone to keeping extras around for employees when she knew what they favored. He'd become practically addicted to her hard cider and took a swallow from his mug.

Marley turned to Delia. "I'm not sure. She said she'd be by tonight, but it's getting late."

Marley's eyes coasted around the table and paused on him. He couldn't read her expression, but she appeared to be considering something. As if on cue, he felt a prickle at the back of his neck and turned to glance over his shoulder toward the entrance. Ginger walked through. She wore a bright red down jacket. When she tossed the hood back, her dark hair fell in loose tousles around her shoulders. She wore black sweater leggings with fluffy white winter boots. As she strode across the room toward them, Cam couldn't keep his eyes off of her, her hips swaying with each step.

She unzipped her jacket and tugged it off on the way, revealing a dove gray sweater that hugged her curves. Just watching her sent anticipation surging through his body.

Don had joined them a few minutes prior and had seated himself beside Cam in the booth, leaving Cam smack in the middle. When Ginger reached the table, Don stood up and gestured for her to sit in his place.

"Don, you don't need to get up just for me," Ginger said, gesturing for Don to sit back down.

Don grinned and shook his head. "I'm heading home. I've got an early start tomorrow." He gave a general wave to the table and made his way out of the restaurant.

Ginger hung her jacket on the corner of the booth and slid in beside Cam. The moment she sat down, his body went taut. He had to force himself to stay focused on the fact they were surrounded by friends and family to keep from giving in to the pounding desire to kiss her again.

"We were just wondering when you'd be by," Marley commented.

Ginger shrugged, her eyes catching his before quickly moving on. "I always show up every few days."

A waitress approached their table and quickly served a glass of wine to Ginger, appearing to know what she wanted without any discussion of the matter. "Do you want to go with the buffet or order something tonight?" the young woman asked.

"I'll take a salmon burger with sweet potato fries," Ginger replied.

"You got it," the waitress said as she quickly filled waters and checked if anyone else needed anything.

After she walked away, conversation turned to the latest local political issue. "I can't believe they're thinking of closing the access to the Flats Beach. Have you heard anything else about it?" Delia asked, directing her question to Ginger.

Ginger rolled her eyes and shifted in her seat as she took a sip of wine. The subtle motion brushed her thigh against his, sending a bolt of electricity through him. *Holy hell. You need to get a hold of yourself, man. All she's doing is sitting beside you.* But Ginger sitting beside him was like nothing he'd ever experienced. His entire body prickled with awareness from her presence. He could feel the heat of her, smell the subtle scent of strawberries and vanilla—she smelled so good he wanted to taste her. He tried to remember if he'd ever noticed how a woman smelled before, and he was fairly certain he hadn't. His attention kicked in somewhere along the way while Ginger was talking.

"I'm not sure what to think. I understand why they're worried about the beach though. Last time I was down there, there were tracks all over the place. I ran into Hannah Winters at Misty Mountain the other day, and she was telling me there've been problems with disrupting the nesting sites for the shorebirds that come through in the summer."

Marley shook her head. "We might not like it, but I don't want to see the beach torn up. I hate that a few assholes ruin things for everyone else."

Conversation moved on to another topic. Cam was only half-paying attention when he felt Ginger glance to him. He turned to her, his eyes colliding with her translucent blue gaze. The murmur of conversation carried on, while the air around them heated. His heart hammered against his ribs, and he couldn't seem to catch his breath. She looked startled and uncertain for a flicker and then she tore her eyes away.

The ebb and flow of conversation continued while Ginger's food arrived. Somewhere along the way, the topic turned to Cam's career in backcountry skiing. He'd only been half-paying attention because of the sheer distraction of Ginger, or he'd have headed the topic off, but he was too late.

"That's why I was so stoked Cam came up here. He's won races all over the world in backcountry skiing, and he's got experience with ski instruction. He's just what we need to get classes going and raise our profile a bit," Gage said with a nod in Cam's direction.

Garrett nudged him. "Yeah, rumor has it you're a bit of a badass on the wild slopes."

Cam shrugged. "I've had a lot of experience, but the backcountry skiing world is pretty small. It's not a main event like in the Olympics, so we don't get as much notice."

Gage grinned. "Cam likes to pretend like it's nothing, but Don knew who he was right away when I mentioned he'd responded to our ad for the job."

Cam prayed too many more questions didn't come up. He'd only spoken with Gage about his brother, so he wasn't sure who else would know. He figured Gage probably mentioned it to Marley. Any conversation about his skiing career was hard to keep Eric removed from. A familiar cold knot of grief tightened in his stomach, and he shifted in his seat.

Garrett caught his eyes again. "A buddy of mine in Seattle is nuts about those backcountry races. He jabbers on about how much harder they are than traditional downhill skiing. I heard about you and your brother from him. He said you two were some of the best around. Is your brother still competing?"

Dread rolled through Cam, immediately followed by a bolt of grief, the pain so acute that he balled his hand in a fist to clench through it. After a breath, he schooled his expression to neutral and shook his head. "Eric died in a car accident last year, but he competed right up until then," he said as calmly as he could.

Quiet fell over the table. Cam didn't dare look around

because he didn't think he could stand what he might see reflected in everyone's gazes. He took a slow breath and a gulp of his beer.

Garrett's almost ever-present half-grin had faded. "I'm sorry. I didn't know about that," he said, his words steady.

Cam nodded. "It's okay. You couldn't have known. I've had some time to get used to it."

He took another breath and allowed his eyes to lift. Gage's gray eyes were warm across the table. He nodded imperceptibly, and Cam knew Gage understood this kind of loss. He couldn't say how or why, but he just knew. A few others made comments similar to Garrett's and somehow conversation made its way past the moment. Cam took another swallow of beer and tried to will away the hollow, tight feeling in his chest. He wondered if he'd ever figure out how to answer innocent questions about Eric without it hurting like hell. One of his hands rested on thigh, and he felt Ginger's hand curl over his. She hooked her thumb in his and squeezed.

He turned his palm, and she laced her fingers in his. The small gesture soothed the ache around his heart. He focused on the warmth of her hand twined with his. The restless, achy feeling inside slowly abated with her touch. He stroked his thumb across the back of her palm. He breathed in and out, absorbing the strength she was imparting. He felt as if she was offering to help carry the burden of his grief and to ease its sharp pain.

* * *

GINGER WALKED into the break room at the school and ducked into the staff bathroom. While she was drying her hands, she could hear the conversation in the break room.

"I signed Justin up for those new ski lessons up at the lodge. The ski instructor is to die for! Have you seen him?"

Ginger recognized Becky Wright's voice. Becky was a third grade teacher at the school. Ginger stepped out of the bathroom and found herself walking to join the three women sitting at the table. Part of her wanted to avoid any gossip about Cam, but she couldn't avoid her curiosity. Becky was seated at the table with Lindsey Holt who taught fourth grade, and Janie Stevens who was probably the most beloved teacher in Diamond Creek. She taught first grade and had a warmth and practicality that endeared her to students and parents alike.

Janie glanced up at Ginger and winked as she sat down beside her. Janie turned to Becky. "Haven't seen him myself, but you're not the first person to mention him to me. Rumor has it he's all kinds of sexy. Diamond Creek's so small, if anyone new shows up like him, he's bound to get attention."

Lindsey chuckled and rolled her eyes. "Becky keeps track for me." She looked over to Ginger. "You must have met him. You're up at the lodge all the time. What's the scoop?"

Ginger felt heat wash through her and willed herself not to blush. She aimed for nonchalant in her reply. "It's Cam Nash. I've met him a few times. He's damn easy on the eyes, but he's also a nice guy. Marley told me the lessons he's set up have been going great." Her mind spun back to last night when she'd learned about his brother. The pain in his eyes had been so sharp, her heart had clenched. She hadn't thought about it when she reached for his hand, but she couldn't have stopped herself. The look in his eyes had reached in and grabbed ahold of her. All she'd wanted was to somehow let him know he wasn't alone. She mentally shook her head. She didn't want to go into that about him, so she kept her comments superficial. "I guess he's a big deal competitor in backcountry ski racing. Gage is stoked to have him here."

Becky grinned. "I might be married, but I like to look. Do you know if he plans to stay around long?"

Ginger schooled her expression to stay neutral. She was still floundering in current of her near overpowering attraction for him and didn't want it to be obvious to others. Becky's question kept dancing through her mind. She couldn't help but wonder. "How would I know?" she asked with a shrug. "I know Gage hopes he does, but I have no idea."

"You never know with people who come here. Either they fall in love with Diamond Creek and want to stay, or they think it's too remote," Janie commented. "If he loves to ski though, it's hard to beat Last Frontier Lodge."

Becky stood from the table and returned a few items to the refrigerator. "Well, aside from the fact he's hot as hell, Justin loved his ski lessons, so I hope he sticks around." At that, she gave a quick wave and headed out of the break room.

Conversation moved on. Ginger checked in with Janie about a student Janie had referred to her while she scarfed down a quick lunch. Lindsey left while they were talking. As they stood up to go, Janie caught her eyes. "You know it's okay to notice a guy, right?"

Ginger prayed she wasn't giving her attraction to Cam away that easily. It was these little moments that scratched at her vulnerability, the vulnerability she thought she'd shielded herself from until Cam crossed her path. She tried to play dumb to dissuade Janie. "Huh?"

Janie was one of her closer friends at work. She put a hand on her hip and rolled her eyes. "You covered it pretty well, but it's obvious to me you think Cam Nash is just as hot as Becky does."

Ginger's cheeks heated. She looked over at Janie with a rueful grin, giving up her efforts at nonchalance about Cam. "Maybe so. He's hard *not* to notice."

Janie grinned. "Well then, notice away!"

As Ginger followed Janie out of the break room and headed back to her office, she wondered if Cam planned to stay in Diamond Creek, or if he was only here for this season. Ski lodges were often filled with temporary, seasonal staff. She got the sense Cam probably didn't know. All the more reason she should steer clear of him. It was bad enough she was trying to accept her attraction to him. She didn't need to worry about the potential messy complications of being into a guy who may or may not be around for very long.

CHAPTER 7

Cam's phone rang as he walked out of the bathroom in his suite. He snagged his phone off the small counter in the kitchen and saw his sister's name flash on the screen.

"Hey Ivy. What's up?"

"Hey Cam! I got your message. Sorry it took a few days for me to call back. I've been so busy with classes and work, I kept forgetting to call until it was too late."

"No worries. I know you're busy. How's school going anyway?"

"It's great, but my schedule's crazy busy. Only one more semester, and I'll be done though."

Cam was so damn proud of Ivy. Ten years younger than him, she'd been a surprise for his parents, a surprise that enriched their world. Ivy was crazy smart and had a giant heart. Even though they were a decade apart, he and Ivy were close. She'd tagged along with him and Eric when they were younger, always full of life, always asking a million questions and up for anything. She was in a graduate program for mechanical engineering at UC Berkeley. Her dream was to design and build entirely self-sustaining energy systems to eliminate the use of fossil fuels. Well, that and building rockets. His sister was a rocket scientist. He loved throwing that detail around. Ivy had held him up in the brutal weeks after Eric died in the accident. She'd been grieving too, but she somehow knew Cam needed her, so she was there one hundred percent. She'd taken a semester off to be with him and their parents.

"That's the end of this semester, right?" Cam asked.

"That's the one! We're not quite to the end of January though, so I've just barely gotten started," Ivy replied with a laugh. "So tell me about Last Frontier Lodge. Mom says you want them to go up for a visit."

"It's great. Seriously. I know you're busy with school, but I hope you can get up here too."

"Maybe I can come during my break in March? Will there still be snow then?"

"Oh yeah. At this elevation, the snow won't even start to melt until later in March. According to Gage, we'll be skiing into April."

"Who's Gage?"

"The guy who owns the lodge. He's a great guy. Honestly, I'd love for you to come so you can see Alaska, but I also think you'd love the people here. Of all the ski lodges I've been to over the years, this one wins for the people."

He could feel Ivy's grin through the phone. "That's awesome, Cam! I don't care how busy I am, I'll get up there."

They chatted causally about a few other topics before Ivy made a comment that made his chest clench. "You know if it's so great there, why don't you think about staying past the season? It could be a good thing for you." Ivy's voice softened. Cam could picture her concerned amber eyes.

He took a slow breath and stared out the window. It was mid-afternoon and he'd come in from hours of grueling work on the trails with Gage. The slopes were dotted with the brightly colored jackets of skiers. He looked to the side where part of Kachemak Bay came into view. The sun glinted off the water and white caps ruffled the surface. The mountains across the bay rose up steeply from the water, their snow-covered flanks giving way to spruce forest dusted with snow. The beauty of this place was breathtaking. Nature had been so generous here with the glory of beautiful, wild coastlines and mountains in the same place. He took another breath and considered Ivy's question. When he'd taken this job, he hadn't thought too far ahead. Eric's death had robbed him of the concept of planning. He was learning there were some upsides to that, namely that he tended to live in the moment and try to focus on that alone.

"Cam?"

Ivy's soft voice nudged him out of his thoughts.

"I'm here," he said, catching his sigh before it slipped out. "I haven't really thought that far ahead," he finally replied to her question about staying past the season. The second he spoke, Ginger danced through his thoughts. He didn't know what to do with the feelings she elicited in him. That brief moment last night when she held his hand was so intimate, he felt strange thinking about it. He was startled by the intimacy and comfort he felt with her. Up to then, he'd been blinded by the blazing hot attraction between them. He mentally shook himself. "I don't know. Maybe I will."

"I just think if you like it that much, it might be worth trying. I worry about you bouncing from ski lodge to ski lodge. Even before Eric died, it was getting close to time for you to slow down and breathe."

Ivy was so open and direct about Eric's death that it hurt sometimes. Yet, it also helped. He thought back to those awkward moments at dinner last night. He could use some of Ivy's matter-of-fact approach sometimes. "I'm not ready to make promises, but I get what you mean. I honestly don't want to bounce around anymore, Ivy, so you don't need to worry about that. I guess I just need a little time to figure things out. I won't be going anywhere soon though, so get up here. Okay?"

Ivy laughed softly. "Well, alright then. I'm glad to hear you're not planning to run all over the world anymore. Maybe I'll see more of you now."

"Hey, don't blame me for that. You're the one who's had her nose buried in books for years. You could use a breather yourself."

Ivy laughed. "Fair enough. So tell me something. I hear there's all kinds of rugged, sexy men in Alaska—I mean, they even have a calendar—but what about women? Met anyone lately?"

Ivy had been on him for years about finding someone. Funny, but she'd never really gotten on Eric's case about it. Eric had been more committed to the lifestyle of a full-time professional skier, which came with endless travel and few commitments. Though Cam had been there with him for most of it, of the brothers, he was more easygoing and a tad less dedicated. To an outsider, it might not have been obvious, but to Ivy, it was. Eric didn't even contemplate the idea of a relationship, while Cam had always figured life would slow down enough at some point for it to happen. Hence, Ivy's occasional pressure on him to look beyond skiing. Her question conjured Ginger in his mind, more specifically the bone-shaking and body-melting kiss of the other night. He wasn't about to tell Ivy about that, but he didn't mind mentioning Ginger. Ivy was the one and only confidant he had in his life now. Even when Eric was alive, Cam wouldn't have talked with him about something like this. That wasn't the nature of their relationship.

"I might have," he finally hedged. "But don't get all crazy. I just met someone who's, I don't know, uh, interesting."

"Interesting is a horrible word to use to describe someone. It's basically useless. I mean, serial killers and librarians could both be described as interesting, but it doesn't tell you a thing about them," Ivy declared. "Tell me about her. What's her name, what's she like, that kind of thing?"

Cam was damn relieved Ivy wasn't here because his face felt hot. Well, his whole body felt hot. Thinking of Ginger automatically did that. "Interesting is not a horrible word, but whatever. I get your point it's not particularly specific. I meant it in the sense that she interests me. Her name is Ginger, and I don't know her that well. She just seems..." *Fucking hot as hell, beautiful, smart, and sweet. Oh and hot as hell.* "...I don't know. She's a friend of Gage's wife, well I guess she's everyone's friend. I don't know her too well, so don't get all crazy over this."

Ivy sighed. "I'm sorry. I didn't mean to get pushy. I'd just love for you to meet someone. You're an awesome guy, and you'd make a great boyfriend. I'm just glad you noticed someone."

Cam chuckled. "Well, let's call it good enough then. Okay?"

"Okay," Ivy said with a laugh. He heard someone's voice in the background. "Oh, crap! I have to go. I forgot I was driving my friend to pick up her car at the mechanic's."

"No worries. Call when you can."

"Okay, I'll check my schedule and text the dates I might be able to come up there. Bye!"

The line clicked dead in his ear before he had a chance to reply. Cam set his phone down on the counter and walked to the windows. He heard an eagle screech in the distance and scanned the trees to find it. He'd yet to get accustomed to the sight of eagles here. He saw one or more every day. Last week, Don had asked him to do the dump run, and he'd been floored when he got there and saw eagles everywhere. There were probably a hundred or more in the area. As he looked over the ski slope, a shadow on the snow alerted him to the eagle taking off from its perch in the trees. Its takeoff was slow, given the immense span of its wings. Once it was in the air, it swooped high and dipped down again before flying out of sight.

With Ivy's question about staying past the season on his mind, he turned away from the window and made his way downstairs to the kitchen. It was on the early side for dinner, but Delia would have something for him to snack on. Gage was generous with staff and meals were part of the deal, so Cam didn't have to worry about scrounging up his own meals. As such, he was probably eating healthier than he had in years because of Delia's cooking.

* * *

GINGER KICKED her feet on the front tire to knock the snow off her boots and climbed inside her car. She'd stopped to pick up the mail before heading home. When she turned the keys to start her car, the engine rumbled, but it didn't catch. After several more tries, she leaned her head back with a sigh. Her mechanic had suggested she replace her battery before this winter, but she'd ignored him. She hadn't wanted to bother with it and preferred to wait until she had to deal with it. It's just that now she *had* to deal with it, and it was annoyingly inconvenient. It was after five in the evening and she just wanted to go home. The wind was whipping viciously off the water today and snow had started to fall within the last hour. Having grown up here, she had a good sense of when it felt like a big storm was brewing. This was one of those days. The air had felt heavy and scented with snow all day. The clouds were thick and foreboding, and the wind simply wouldn't quit. With a sigh, she fumbled in her purse for her phone and quickly dialed her mother's number. When she didn't get an answer, she left a quick message and stared down at her phone. Usually, the next person she'd call would be Marley, but Marley was literally due to have her baby any day now. Ginger didn't want to drag her all the way to town for a ride when the weather could get worse.

The sound of tires rolling across the snow-packed parking lot drew her attention. A black truck pulled up beside her. With the snow, she couldn't quite see who it was, so she rolled down her window to find Cam waving to her. He rolled his window down as well. "Hey there, how's it going?" he asked.

"Fine. You?" While she managed to speak to him, a hot flush washed through her at seeing him again and warmth curled around her heart at having him stop to say hello. That's how silly she was over him—him simply greeting her fed straight into her annoyingly hopeful heart.

He shrugged. "Busy, but good. Thought I'd say hi when I saw your car."

A blast of icy wind whipped through her car window and she flinched. Ginger pondered for a second. The smart thing would be to ask Cam for a ride, but her pride held her back, along with a prick of apprehension. She was betwixt and between about her stupid attraction to him. It annoyed her to keep hearing other women comment on how handsome he was and made her feel she was just like everyone else. Diamond Creek was a small world. Someone like Cam couldn't breeze into town without being noticed. Another gust of icy air whooshed through her window, making the decision for her. She wasn't going to sit here and wait to see if her mother called her back. She wanted to be home where it was warm, although her heart fluttered at the thought of asking him for help.

"Actually, my battery's dead. Would you mind giving me a ride home? I don't live far from here and it's the same direction as the lodge."

Cam's brows hitched. "Of course not. It's too damn cold

for you to sit around in this. You want me to try to jump the battery?"

"Not now. My mechanic told me months ago this battery was on its last legs. It's freezing out, and I don't know if it will work. I'd rather just hitch a ride and figure it out tomorrow before the snow gets too heavy."

He nodded. "Okay then. Come on over."

She grabbed her purse and phone, and made sure her car was locked before she scurried around to the passenger side of his truck. He swung the door open from the inside when she reached it. In the brief moment from her car to his truck, she was shivering from the cold and her cheeks stung from the wind driven snow.

She climbed in swiftly and closed the door. In seconds, the warmth of his truck sifted around her. She rubbed her arms and glanced over. "Thank you. It's freezing out there. I just wasn't up for trying to do the whole jump start thing."

He grinned. "Me neither. I would've done it if you wanted, but it's brutal out there. So where to?"

She quickly gave him directions. As he drove along, the snow picked up pace, flying fast and furious against his windshield.

"Damn, looks like we're in for a hell of a storm tonight. I said as much to Gage this morning. I don't know how to explain it, but the air smells a certain way when snow's coming."

She glanced to him with a grin, almost giddy to find this detail in common. "I said the same thing! It's hard to describe unless you know what it's like." On the heels of her words, the defensive part of herself reared up, reminding her not to be ridiculous. So they both happened to notice how the air smelled before it snowed? Following that, her heart, which was getting rather chatty lately, pointed out it wasn't so bad to enjoy a small connection.

Cam chuckled. "Snow is snow. I might not have lived in

Alaska before, but I've spent most of my life in places where it snows a lot." He slowed as he approached one of the few stoplights in Diamond Creek.

Ginger could feel the wheels go into a brief skid as he came to a stop. He appeared unruffled by the slick road. While they waited for the light to change, a few cars passed through the intersection without incident before a truck came through and started to turn. The driver lost control and the truck spun out and bumped the curb. The truck came to a bouncing stop. The driver waited a moment and carefully maneuvered off the curb before driving away.

Cam shook his head, but didn't say anything. The snow pelted against the windshield. In the few minutes since they'd left the post office, the snow had steadily gotten heavier and picked up the pace. By this point, visibility was only a few feet ahead. When the light changed, he started driving slowly through the intersection.

"I'm taking it slow, so I hope you're not in a hurry," he said.

"Seeing as I'd still be sitting in my car at the post office if it weren't for you giving me a ride, you definitely don't need to worry about me complaining about how slow you're driving. Taking it slow is the smart thing right now. It's getting bad pretty fast." No matter how many years she'd driven in rough weather, it always made her a little anxious. Cam's steady presence soothed her, which also flustered her because she didn't like how much she enjoyed his confident, calm manner.

The rest of the drive was quiet, save the wind howling outside and the incessant sound of snow drumming against the windshield. He eventually made it to her house, following her earlier directions precisely. He carefully turned into her driveway. The snow was piling up, so she guided him to where to park. She looked his way and wondered what to say. The words that came out surprised her. She most certainly wasn't thinking, yet she couldn't help but want to hunker down with him to wait the storm out.

"Want to come in? You might be better off waiting the storm out here for a bit before you head up the hill to the lodge."

Uh, what the hell are you thinking? I'm thinking the weather's awful and I don't want to see him drive away in this. I'll be worried until I know he makes it back to the lodge. Oh right, you're worried about him. Maybe so, but it's more than that and you know it.

Ginger sighed internally. Cam had this amazing ability to turn off the sensible part of her brain. She could tell herself she was worried about the weather, and she legitimately was, but the part of her that got bold and invited him to come in was the part that wanted Cam like she'd never wanted any man.

She looked out the window into the swirl of blinding snow. The wind was flying in hard off the water and blowing the snow sideways. With her house situated on the bluff overlooking the bay, when storms came in, the house tended to bear the brunt of the wind with little to offer protection. When she turned back to Cam, he was staring out at the snow as well. His profile was silhouetted in the shadowed car. The strong, clean lines of his face held her gaze. When he glanced her way, a bolt of need shot through her and butterflies amassed in her belly.

He nodded, and she forgot what she'd last said.

"If you don't mind, it's probably better if I wait a bit to see if this slows down. I'd rather not drive at a crawl in this snow. The visibility's close to none."

Oh yeah. She'd invited him to come in and stay until the snow slowed down. It occurred to her this storm didn't appear to have any plans for slowing down. If her guess was right, they were only at the beginning. Her mind dodged away from what that could mean as far as Cam waiting it out.

"Let's get inside then," she said quickly. She tugged her gloves on and threw her hood up before climbing out.

They trudged through the snow to her front door. Her porch light had come on automatically since it was set on a timer. The soft glow of the light was a beacon in the falling darkness and driving snow. She pointlessly tried to kick the snow off her boots before she stepped inside, but she immediately picked up more snow the moment she set her foot down again.

After they got inside, she put her boots by the heater to dry off and hung her coat up, insisting he do the same. She flicked the lights on in the living room and kitchen and turned on an outside light. It illuminated the snow on the other side of the windows, lighting it up like falling glitter.

She went straight to the kitchen and gestured for Cam to sit at the small round table in the corner. "Coffee? Tea? Or maybe you'd rather have a beer."

"Got any of Delia's hard cider?" he countered with a grin.

She burst out laughing. "She's got you hooked too, huh?"

He nodded emphatically.

She turned and walked into the small pantry off to the side of the kitchen. "Hang on, let me see. Delia gave me a few quarts of it a while ago. I'm not sure if I have any left."

After rearranging a messy shelf, she found two quarts of Delia's beloved hard cider behind some flour and a bag of tortilla chips. She snagged both jugs and the chips on her way out. As she came out of the pantry, she heard the distinct sound of George bounding across the floor and into the kitchen. He paused once he came through the archway and rested on his haunches. His wide blue eyes landed on Cam. Cam's legs were stretched out in front of him with one foot resting atop the other. George sniffed the air and then took several hops to land beside Cam's feet. He immediately set to sniffing them curiously. After several seconds, he looked up and leapt straight onto Cam's lap.

Cam chuckled and glanced to Ginger.

"That's George. He's my house rabbit. He's super friendly. He's kind of like a cat, house trained and all."

Cam looked down and stroked his hand across George's back. George immediately leaned into his touch and rubbed his head against Cam's chest.

"I found some cider," Ginger offered, holding the two jugs aloft. "Let me heat it up though. Delia swears we can't use the microwave for that, so it'll take a few minutes on the stove."

Cam grinned, still petting George. "Awesome. Until I started at Last Frontier Lodge, I couldn't even tell you if I'd had hard cider before. I must have because it's the kind of thing they serve at ski lodges, but hers is out of this world. Do you know what she does to make it so amazing?"

She shook her head. "Nope. It's her mother's recipe. She won't give it to anyone. That's fine with me because she gives it out left and right. You must be enjoying the food there. That's part of the deal for staff, right?"

"Yup. Gage is the most generous lodge manager I've ever known. He doesn't sweat the small stuff and makes sure we get the benefits of living at the lodge. I've been all over and some places can be downright stingy. It's nice to be at Last Frontier. Gage makes it easy. Delia's food might be the best side benefit I've ever had."

"It's not like you have to wonder why so many locals are up there all the time," Ginger said with a wry grin as she poured the cider into a stainless steel pot and turned on the propane burner. She adjusted the heat to low, per Delia's instructions, and sat down across from Cam at the table. George lifted his head from where he'd been rubbing it against Cam's chest and eyed her. He appeared to be considering whether to remain on Cam's lap or come greet her. He finally leapt down and immediately bounced up onto her lap.

"Hey George." She petted him and allowed him to nuzzle her cheeks. He settled on her lap and rested while she stroked his back. She looked over at Cam. "I'd always wanted a rabbit when I was little, so I finally got one after my divorce." Oops. She hadn't meant to go there. The explanation was entirely true, but she didn't really want to open any doors to questions about her short-lived joke of a marriage.

"Oh." There was a long pause. "How long have you had him?"

It occurred to her that by answering his question, she'd be sort of telling him how long ago her divorce was. She hated the whole divorce thing because no matter what anyone said, there was this weird social thing around divorces. They represented this massive mistake. What she wished was to be able to go back in time and figure out that Tony wasn't worth her youthful love *before* she married him. She mentally shook her head and tried to focus on the moment. She had tons of baggage around her marriage and divorce. She didn't need to go thinking Cam was reading into anything. All he'd asked was how long she'd had George.

"I've had him for two years. Rabbits make great pets. He bounces around the house and eats vegetables. In the summer, I let him outside when I'm home. He's on the small side for a lop-eared rabbit—he'd be lunch for an eagle, so it's not good to let him out unless I'm home. I try to get him to go out in the winter, but he's kind of a prima donna. He's not a fan of the cold and he hates snow."

George lifted his head and eyed her as if he knew she was talking about him. A gust of wind blew outside, sending snow pelting against the windows. George turned toward the sound and bounced off of her lap. He hopped over for a drink from his water bowl and then leapt up onto the windowsill to stare outside at the swirling snow. The wind had picked up its pace since they came in, the snow following suit. Cam likely wouldn't be heading to the lodge anytime soon. Ginger found it hard not to stare at him. Just being here in a room with him and the air felt alive, snapping with the electric current buzzing between them.

Restless, she stood up and walked to the refrigerator to look inside. "How about I make some dinner? I'm not a phenomenal cook like Delia, but I've been told I'm halfway decent."

She let the refrigerator door fall closed and leaned against the counter. Her kitchen was small, but the archway lent it a more open feel. The round table sat by the windows. Cobalt blue tiled counters lined two walls with a doorway sized opening into the pantry. A porcelain sink sat in the center of one counter while a stainless steel oven and stove were on the other wall. She looked to Cam. "Any preferences for dinner?"

He shrugged. "You don't have to cook just because I'm here."

"I'm cooking for myself because I'm starving. Consider it a selfish act. Plus, let's be real," she nudged her chin toward the window and the snow pinging against it "...you're not going anywhere anytime soon. You might as well eat. I can't let you starve."

His amber eyes held hers for a few beats. All he had to do was look at her and heat unfurled inside, spiraling outward from her center. Her breath hitched and she tried not to notice how handsome he was. Between those eyes, which were hot enough to melt her, and his insanely hot body, it was no wonder his mere presence in Diamond Creek stirred up gossip. She'd like to think she'd be immune, but she was far from it. She was practically a puddle around him.

"I'll eat whatever you want to cook. I'm easy that way," he finally replied.

She pushed away from the counter with her hips and opened the refrigerator again. She spied a few tomatoes and some fresh Parmesan cheese she'd picked up the other day. "How about pasta with fresh marinara sauce?"

"Sounds good. Can I help with anything?"

She grabbed the tomatoes and set them on the counter. "Nope. I got it. Let's check the cider though. It should be warming up."

She quickly lifted the lid on it and steam rose from the pot, along with the scent of cider and spices. She lifted two mugs off the hooks that hung from under one of the cabinets and ladled them full of hard cider. She handed one over to Cam who took a gulp and sighed with pleasure. "Damn, this is the best."

Ginger took a swallow and nodded. "This is Delia's magic. You should hear Garrett go on about it. Delia swears he only wanted to marry her for this," she said with a soft laugh.

Cam shook his head. "Nah. Garrett might love her cider, but that man is crazy in love with her."

"I know. It's so obvious when you see them together." She experienced a twinge of sadness. Not because she wasn't happy for Delia and Garrett. She was ecstatic for them, especially knowing Delia had all but written off love. Life as a single mother didn't leave much room for men, but Garrett had found a way straight to Delia's heart. Ginger's sadness came from that place within her that had been so stupidly blind about her former husband. She loved seeing her friends find love, but sometimes she had to remind herself she was better off on her own.

Ginger set her cider down and pulled out a pot for the

pasta and another for the sauce. She quickly got water boiling and stepped into the pantry for some tomato paste. In just a few minutes, she had added enough water to the tomato paste for sauce and set it on low heat while she chopped tomatoes and added spices to it.

While she cooked, they somehow managed to casually talk. Cam asked her questions about Diamond Creek, and she asked about places he'd traveled. She tried to be careful and avoid asking about his brother. It was so clear the other night that his grief over his brother's death was still fresh. After talking a bit about his travels, he looped back to her.

"So you grew up here?" he asked.

"Born and raised in Diamond Creek. Alaska's full of transplants, so you won't find too many people who've been here most of their lives. I moved away for college and grad school, but I came home after that. It might be small, but Diamond Creek's an amazing place. We have some of the most beautiful scenery in the world. With the tourists that flow through here, we have great restaurants and shopping. When I was away, I missed being in a small town. Sometimes it feels like everybody knows your business, but they care. I'll admit when I was in high school, I couldn't wait to move away. You know? The whole grass is always greener thing. After over six years away, I was more than ready to come back."

Cam nodded. "I can see that. It's nice you have a place that means something to you. Pretty much since I graduated high school, I've been traveling every few months and more. When I was in college, I was already competing, so I'd take weekends and travel to races. Once I graduated, that was my life. Sponsorships and prize money supported me." His eyes clouded, but he took a breath and continued. "Eric took it more seriously than me, so he was almost always on the road. Before he died, I kept thinking I'd plan to back down from racing full-time and figure it out. I see someone like you and I kinda wish I had a place like Diamond Creek to anchor me."

"Where's your family?"

"Utah. Small town outside of Salt Lake City. My dad runs a gear shop, and my mom's a librarian at the local library. I've been skiing as long as I can remember. I didn't set out to compete, but I followed my brother into it. Next thing I knew, it was my whole life. We used to live in Salt Lake City before that, so I didn't have my whole childhood in one place like you. Makes it harder to feel too attached to a place."

She gave the sauce a stir and added the garlic she'd crushed. "Be careful. Diamond Creek has this bizarre effect on people where they come to visit and end up staying forever."

He chuckled and took another gulp of cider. "That might not be all bad."

Her heart did a funny little flip flop in her chest. The mere idea Cam might be here more than temporarily sent hope tap-dancing in her mind, trying to convince her it might not be too crazy to think she could try a relationship again. There was a gigantic maybe attached to that idea. *Maybe? Have you completely lost it? I thought you weren't going to worry about this attraction, like Marley said. Cam's sexy as all hell, but it doesn't mean you have to turn it into more than it is. Yeah, but it feels like there's more.* That last thought was the barely audible voice of her heart. It was hard to hear over the rather loud and authoritative voice of her rational brain, the part of her that held her together and got her through the humiliating months after her marriage was revealed for what it was. After years of being shouted over, her heart was trying to make its voice heard. She mentally batted the thoughts away and got busy checking the pasta.

A while later, she stood from the table and carried her plate to the dishwasher. Cam leaned back in his chair and set his fork down. "Wow. That was really good. I didn't realize how hungry I was." He lifted his mug as if to take a sip and looked inside before glancing up with a rueful grin. "Empty." He pushed his chair back and stood, carting his plate to the dishwasher as well.

A gust of wind rattled the windows. George bounced off the windowsill in response and hopped past them into the living room and up the stairs. Cam watched him go with a grin. "He just hops around, huh?"

"Oh yeah. That's pretty much what he does. He has a few places he likes to nap and some toys he plays with here and there."

Ginger closed the dishwasher. "More cider?"

"Definitely." He handed over his mug.

She filled his and then another for herself. Another gust of wind blasted against the house. Snow pinged rapidly on the windows.

"I'll be surprised if we keep power the way it's blowing out there," she said, realizing she'd better accept the fact Cam was likely here for the night. In good conscience, she couldn't expect him to drive anywhere in this. A part of her went taut with anticipation, her heart practically cheering. Yet another part of her was plain terrified. She was torn by the depth of her attraction to him and so unsettled by how easily her emotions had become tangled in her desire. Her chest tightened with anxiety. She wanted him so much, it shook her to her core. After sitting through a dinner with him, it was all she could do to breathe. Her pulse raced, her low belly fluttered every time his amber gaze landed on her, and heat suffused her. She prayed she wasn't too flushed.

She handed him his cider and walked past him into the living room. "Have a seat," she said, gesturing in the direction of the couch. She was somewhat minimalist when it came to furnishings and decoration. She had a charcoal gray sectional in the corner of the small living room. With the soapstone woodstove taking up the center, this allowed a view out the windows during daytime and a view of the fire at night if she had one. The television was mounted on the one portion of the back wall that didn't contain windows. She had a few paintings on the walls and a muted purple throw rug on the floor. She set her cider down on the end table by the couch and knelt by the woodstove to start a fire. Just as she struck a match to light the fire, a vicious gust of wind rattled the windows again and the power went out. It flickered on and then off again. The flames took hold in the tinder under the logs she'd set inside the woodstove, offering a soft glow in the dark room.

"Saw that coming," Cam commented, his gravelly voice sending a prickle of awareness up her spine.

Ginger brushed her hands off and stood. "I've got some candles scattered around. Let me light them, so we can at least see. Even if the power doesn't come back on, this woodstove will keep the whole house warm."

"Need some help?"

"Sure. Why don't you get the candles in here lit?" she asked, gesturing to a few candles strategically placed on the end tables and in the corners on decorative stands. She snagged another long match from the materials she kept by the woodstove, passed it through the flames inside and handed it to him. "I'll go get some more candles I keep in the kitchen."

"Got it," he replied, quickly moving around the room and lighting candles.

She strode into the kitchen to pull out a few emergency candles and left one burning in the kitchen and carried the rest out to the living room. They were the wide base type that required no holder. By the time they had all the candles lit, the living room was aglow in soft light.

With the wind howling outside, Ginger poked her head out the front door to see the state of the snow and promptly shut it. It was a white out. A good foot or more had accumulated in the time they'd reached her house.

"Okay, you're here for the night. It's horrible out there."

Cam had returned to the couch and was taking a swallow of cider. He set it down with a satisfied sigh. "I hope you don't mind. If you do, I can leave. I could make it to the lodge in this weather. I've had plenty of experience driving in snow."

She walked to the couch and sat down with a roll of her eyes. "So have I, but I'm not stupid. I'm not going to let you drive in this. You can't see a thing out there." She paused and looked over at him. He sat at an angle from her. He'd relaxed into the couch. Even in the dim light, she could see the etched muscles of his chest and abdomen through his cotton shirt. He appeared to live in cotton jersey shirts that hugged his drool-worthy body. He usually paired those with faded jeans. When she saw him skiing, he didn't tend to go for the flashy bright colors many skiers did. He stuck with black. Right now, in the quiet of her living room with a fire crackling in the woodstove and the wind and snow swirling around them outside, it felt like they were in a cocoon. Her pulse kicked up a notch, and that inconvenient desire flared. His eyes held hers, and she felt as if he could see right through her to the wild desire beating its wings inside.

Restless and desperate to distract herself from the feelings Cam elicited, she set her cider down and tugged open a small drawer in the end table. "Cards!" she declared.

CHAPTER 8

Cam couldn't help but laugh when Ginger triumphantly slapped the messy pile of cards between them on the couch. They'd been playing for a while now, and he'd promptly discovered Ginger didn't mess around when it came to cards. He'd played his share of various card games over the years, but didn't have much of a competitive streak for it. He managed to beat her in a few games of rummy, but otherwise she mostly trounced him. He couldn't remember the last time he'd laughed this much. Nor could he remember ever being this attracted to anyone. Being in close quarters in the accidentally romantic candle-light sent lust coursing through him. Ginger had seemed tense at points earlier in the evening, but once they started playing cards, she relaxed. She was sharp, funny, and so damn beautiful, he had a hard time staying focused. Little did she know that was half the reason she was beating him so many times. His mind was mostly dwelling on the plump curve of her bottom lip and the generous curves of her breasts, which he glimpsed each time she leaned over. She wore a fitted cotton v-neck shirt that revealed the shadowed valley between her breasts.

He had all kinds of reasons why he shouldn't let anything more happen between them, but at the moment, those reasons were weak and insubstantial in the face of his desire for her. He took a gulp of air and tried to draw reason in along with a breath, but all he could see was Ginger gathering up the cards with her hair falling around her shoulders as she leaned forward. She glanced up, her blue eyes widening when she met his gaze. The air around them sizzled with heat.

The cards slipped out of her hands and tumbled to the floor. His weak hold on reason dissolved when she scooted closer to him. "Oh hell, I'm kissing you again," she said just before she slid her hand around the back of his neck.

Not only did he not bother resisting, he crashed his lips against hers the second her hand curled around his neck. The heat between them went from embers flicking sparks to an all out flaming fire. Her lips were so soft and so full. The feel of them against his was intoxicating. He'd been resting in the corner of the sectional. He leaned back and cupped his hands under her hips, pulling her onto his lap. She didn't hesitate and turned into him, gasping when he pulled her closer. On her gasp, he delved his tongue into the warm sweetness of her mouth. Holy hell. Kissing her shredded his control. The combination of her boldness and sweetness and the feel of her lips and soft curves against him nearly drove him mad. He was rock hard and his pulse was pounding through him.

Ginger's tongue tangled with his. She kissed with wild abandon. Every stroke of her tongue against his pushed him further over the edge. When she shifted in his lap and straddled him, want coiled within and lashed at him. He could feel the heat of her against his cock, despite the two layers of clothing between them—his and hers. She settled her hips against him and moaned into his mouth when he arched into her. He broke free from her mouth, desperate for a taste of that hint of strawberry and vanilla her skin carried. He blazed a trail down her neck with his lips, teeth and tongue. With every kiss and nip, she rolled her hips against him. Bolts of lust shot through him again and again.

All restraint gone, he dragged his tongue down into the valley between her breasts and slipped his hands under her shirt. Her skin was hot to the touch. All he wanted was to feel more of her. He shoved her shirt up, tearing his lips from her skin just long enough to yank it off and toss it on the floor. He paused to look at her. Her hair was mussed and fell in a loose tangle around her face. Her lips were swollen from their kisses. Her breasts rose and fell in unison with her breath, which came in rapid pants, matching his own shallow breathing. She wore a lacy black bra, which barely covered her full breasts. Glimpses of her pink nipples peeked at him through the lace.

With lust beating its drum inside of him, he forced his eyes up. He barely had any control, but he knew if he gave into the driving need to tear the rest of her clothes off, taste every inch of her and sink inside her, he needed to know she was as sure as he was. When he met her eyes, his heart clenched and a disconcerting sense of intimacy washed over him. He could hardly think for the pounding of his heart. Something flashed in the depths of her eyes.

"I'm not so sure I can stop if we go much further, so tell me now if you don't want this," he managed to say, his words rough and raw.

Her breath came out with a choked laugh. "I want this," she said, her words husky.

* * *

GINGER SAT THERE, straddling Cam's strong thighs and feeling the pulse of his rock-hard cock against the center of her desire. The weak voice of reason within her appreciated Cam's attempt to give her a chance to back out. Hell no. She wasn't backing out of this. Maybe she'd tried to persuade herself she didn't need men and didn't need sex. But right here, right now, she wanted Cam fiercely and she wasn't about to deny herself more of the pleasure she sensed he could give her. For crying out loud, she was on the verge of an orgasm sitting astride him with most of her clothes on. As she stared at him, her mind spun, trying to recall if she had any condoms anywhere if he didn't happen to have some. Just when she was about to ask him, she remembered she'd hosted a bachelorette party for one of the teachers at school and someone had brought a bag full of sex toys, which conveniently included condoms. They'd been left here, and she'd stuffed them in the bathroom cabinet.

After he spoke, she couldn't help the laugh that tumbled out. As if she could even consider stopping. "I want this" fell from her lips before thought could prevent it.

As soon as she answered him, his mouth hooked at the corner in that slow grin she was coming to adore. He lifted a hand and traced her lips before dragging his finger down along her throat, across her collarbone and dipping into the valley between her breasts before he circled one of her nipples. Her nipples were so tight, they were on the verge of pain. She needed him to give her relief, and oh did he ever. On the heels of his finger circling her nipple, he caught them both between his thumbs and forefinger and rolled them. Pleasure shot through her. Her head fell back on a moan when his lips closed around one. The moist heat of his mouth through her lacy bra drove her nearly wild. His tongue swirled a wet circle before he lightly nipped. A cry fell from her lips. When he moved to her other breast, the cool air against the wet lace notched the heat inside even higher.

Frantic, she shoved at his shirt, yanking it up and over his head. He tore his lips away and flicked his finger under the clasp of her bra. When her breasts tumbled loose, she curled her arms around his shoulders, savoring the flex of his muscles under her hands and pulled herself against him. She sighed in relief at the feel of his hard body against the softness of hers. His head fell against the back of the couch, his eyes catching hers. His amber gaze melted her. The air around them shimmered, the heat between them sizzling.

His palms stroked down her sides, his thumbs coasting over her nipples, and came to rest at her hips. He flicked the button on her jeans and slid her zipper down. She rolled her hips against him, pleasure shooting through her as his cock nudged against her. She shimmied off of him. He arched a brow in question as she dashed away. "Hang on," she called over her shoulder as she raced into the bathroom. She flung the cabinet under the sink open and dug through until she found what she was looking for. She yanked the condoms out and raced back into the living room.

Cam sat on the couch, his chest gleaming in the candlelit room. Her pulse, which had barely slowed, instantly rocketed wildly. She paused in front of him. He arched a brow again, and she held up the condoms. His eyes widened and then he chuckled. It occurred to her she should be nervous, considering she was about to have sex for the first time in over two years. Yet, with him, she just didn't feel nervous. It helped that the attraction between them was too overwhelming for her rational brain to have any say. She tossed the strip of condoms to the table by the couch and moved to straddle him again.

His hands stilled her when he curled them around her hips. "Wait," he said gruffly.

He hooked his fingers over the waistband of her jeans and dragged them down swiftly. She kicked them loose and stood before him in nothing but her oh-so-practical black cotton underwear. She could hardly hear over the pounding of her heart when he cupped her mound and stroked a finger across the cotton between her legs. Her breath caught and a moan fell from her lips. He set to stroking back and forth, back and forth, all the while she nearly melted into a puddle. She was slick with need. He finally dragged her underwear down and slipped his fingers into her drenched folds.

In seconds, her knees buckled with his teasing. He caught her with one arm and dragged her onto the couch. Before she knew what was happening, he'd pushed her back and shifted his position to bring his mouth against her. She went from frantic to desperate. Pure pleasure whipped through her as he explored her folds with his lips and tongue, stroking his fingers into her channel again and again. Everything became a blur of sensation as her channel throbbed and he swirled his tongue over the nub of her desire. When she cried out at her sharp release, he moved seamlessly up her body. His lips mapped their way up. She grabbed at him, tearing his jeans open and shoving them down with her hands and feet.

He stretched across her and snagged the condoms she'd tossed on the table. In seconds, she heard the tear of foil. He rolled the condom on and settled his hips against her. His elbows bracketed her face, and he whispered her name. She opened her eyes and lost herself in his amber gaze. Her heart squeezed at the intimacy she saw there. She knew it was reflected in her own eyes. For a split second, fear darted through her. But the moment held her steady, too powerful to allow something else to take over. She felt him at her entrance and arched against him. In a deep surge, he sheathed himself within her. She gasped at the feeling of fullness. She was tight because it had been a while, and he was, well, he was more than she'd expected. He held still for a long moment, his eyes locked to hers. Her body finally eased and relaxed around him.

She curled her legs around his hips when he began to move. She felt every inch of him as he pulled back and surged inside—again and again and again. Her breath became ragged as the pressure within her spun tighter and tighter. She thundered to the edge of another orgasm with each stroke. His hips drummed into hers when she cried out at the hot rush of another climax. He followed her over the edge with a muffled shout as his body went rigid and his head fell into her shoulder. He shuddered against her, his shudders echoing hers.

They lay like that for several moments, their breath the only sound in the quiet room. The sound of the snowstorm outside gradually filtered into her awareness. Cam slowly lifted his head. His eyes met hers, and the moment was so intimate, it almost hurt. She didn't know what she'd expected, but it wasn't this deep connection. She managed to keep breathing when he dipped his head and brought his lips to hers. The kiss was brief, but she felt it through her entire body. He slowly pulled away and untangled himself. He stood and walked toward the bathroom. She couldn't help but admire his body. In the candlelit room, his skin gleamed. Every inch of him was sculpted muscle, a pure specimen of athlete. When he returned from the bathroom, he'd disposed of his condom. He paused by the couch.

"Since we already decided it was silly for me to try to drive, where are we sleeping?" he asked, his voice husky.

She leaned up on her elbows and glanced around the room. The woodstove would keep the whole house from freezing, but anywhere outside of the living room would be chilled. "One section of this couch folds out. We should just sleep down here. It won't be horrible upstairs in my bedroom, but it won't be too cozy either."

"Sounds good to me."

It occurred to her that perhaps she should feel self-conscious standing up completely bare in front of him, but she wasn't. She stood and gathered her clothes, while he did the same. The mundane moment sent her heart in a slow flip. In the heat of the moment, she could forget to think about what was happening. Right now, the intimacy between them felt quite real...and terrifying. She took a breath and swatted the thoughts away. Thinking was most definitely *not* helpful right now. She looked over at him when she was about to get dressed. "I'm going to run upstairs and get something more comfortable. I can probably find some clothes for you."

His eyes widened.

"Oh, it's nothing weird. I used to help coach the local community baseball team and have boxes of men's and women's t-shirts and sweatpants in all sizes."

At his chuckle, she scurried up the stairs to her bedroom. After she grabbed a soft cotton shirt and leggings for herself, she rummaged through the closet and found the box of men's stuff for him. Rather than trying to find something for him, she carted it downstairs with George hopping down the stairs behind her. Cam quickly dug through and found a pair of gray sweatpants and matching t-shirt with the DC Batters logo.

"DC Batters?" he asked.

"Diamond Creek Batters. We were the local champs for two seasons. Don't make fun," she said with a grin.

A while later, they'd tugged out the fold out portion of the couch and curled up on it with George. Cam had played a few more hands of cards with her, and she'd suspiciously wondered if he was letting her win, but she didn't really care. As she drifted off to sleep, all she knew was his arm resting on her waist and his thumb tracing lazy circles over her belly. She was warm and more relaxed than she'd been in years. His hand gradually stilled and his breathing became even.

CHAPTER 9

When Cam woke with Ginger's warm body curled against his, he rolled his head to the side to look out the windows. The sun was shining brightly, glittering on the surface of Kachemak Bay. Ginger's house was situated on a bluff above the bay, so her view of the ocean and mountains across was much closer than what he saw from the lodge. The storm had passed and left close to three feet of snow behind. Sometime during the night, the power had come back on. Ginger rolled over and pushed herself up on an elbow. One look at her tousled hair, sleepy blue eyes, and the lush curve of her breasts as the sheet slipped down and his body was instantly on notice. Just when he was contemplating if he'd completely lost his mind, her phone rang. She rolled over and wrapped one of the blankets around her as she shuffled over to the kitchen. Seconds later, she squealed.

"Marley's on the way to the hospital! She's having her baby!"

The next little while flew by with Ginger frantically showering and getting dressed. Gage called Cam to report the same news. While Ginger was getting ready to leave, Cam headed out to clear the snow off of his truck. He planned to drop her off at the hospital and then stop by the post office to replace the battery in her car. A quick call to Don, and Don agreed to follow him over to the hospital to drop off Ginger's car later. While he was brushing snow off his truck, Ginger's neighbor swung through her driveway with the plow.

Ginger came flying out the door, a red scarf whipping over her shoulder in the lingering wind from the storm. She skidded to his side, her eyes bright blue in the sun. "I have to go. Do you mind feeding George before you go? I just remembered I forgot to do that."

Cam stood there, still trying to wrap his brain around the fact he'd had the best sex of his life last night with the woman standing in front of him. He had no idea what to do with this unexpected development. Meanwhile, a part of him was relieved Ginger had to race off because it bought him some respite from the confusion tumbling around in his brain. He forced himself to pay attention. "I think you forgot you don't have your car. How about you take my truck? I'll feed George and have Don come by and pick me up."

Her hand flew to her mouth. "I can't believe I forgot! You sure you don't mind?"

"Not at all. Go be with Marley. I'll take care of George and have your car dropped off later. What do I feed him?"

"His veggies are in the fridge. I keep his pellets in the pantry in a bin on the floor. Just fill the two small bowls in the bin and leave them out. His water bowl is on the floor in the kitchen." She paused and glanced around. Before he realized what was happening, she flung her arms around him. "Thank you for taking care of everything!"

His arms came around her reflexively. When he looked into her face, her smile was wide and her eyes glittering.

Once again, his brain appeared to have turned off because without a single thought, he leaned forward and kissed her. For a brief kiss, it was so hot, it nearly singed him. Her lips were plump and soft under his, warm against the contrast of the icy air around them. She exclaimed into his mouth and next thing he knew, his tongue was tangling with hers. By the time he managed to pull back, lust was humming through him. He forced himself to remember she was on the way to be with her best friend who was having a baby. He eased his hold and she slipped down to the ground, her boots crunching on the snow.

She reached for the door handle and looked to him. "Are you going to the hospital?"

He shook his head. "Nope. Gage already asked me to be on duty on the slopes. I'll run inside to feed George and wait for Don to come pick me up."

She nodded quickly and climbed into his truck. With a wave, she backed up and drove away. He returned inside to feed George. George was expectantly waiting in the kitchen. He bounded to Cam's side and followed him into the pantry, while Cam followed Ginger's instructions to feed him.

A while later, Cam tugged his ski gear on and walked out onto the back deck at the lodge. Don had picked him up at Ginger's house, and they'd quickly gone to the post office to replace her battery and drop her car off at the hospital. He'd helped himself to the breakfast buffet and was ready for several hours of checking on skiers who needed assistance and essentially cruising around. With the lodge completely booked, everything carried on there. Don had headed to the top of the slopes to clear snow around the lift landings.

Cam grabbed his skis and hopped on the lift once he was ready. When he arrived at the main landing, an area where four different slopes could be accessed, he found Don hard at work clearing the snow around the small warming hut. Cam skied to Don's side.

"Need some help?"

Don glanced up, his weathered face crinkling with his smile. "You know, I'd like to say no, but I'm slower than I used to be. If you don't mind helping for a few minutes, we can have this cleared pretty quick."

"No problem." Cam loosened his bindings and stepped out of his skis. He snagged the extra shovel hanging high on the side of the small cabin and immediately got to work shoveling. In short order, the cabin was cleared, so skiers could access it if needed. Don stepped inside and checked the propane heater and returned to Cam's side where he was adjusting the bindings on his skis.

"That was a big help. You headed to do your rounds?" Don asked.

"Yup. I'll loop through every slope. I've got my radio, so if you see anything, holler at me."

Don chuckled. "You got it. Any word on Marley?"

Cam shook his head. "I got the call she was in labor and they were headed to the hospital, but that's the last I heard."

Don nodded slowly. "Could be a while before we hear anything." At that, he stepped to the snowmobile he used for travel on the mountain. "I'll see you later," he said with a wave.

The snowmobile roared when Don started it. Cam watched Don zip away, the sound of the snowmobile's engine slowly fading. He took a gulp of cold air and glanced around. Today was sheer heaven for a skier. The storm last night had left behind a dense base of fluffy snow. For backcountry skiing, it was like skiing on a cloud. For downhill skiing, this kind of snow afforded cushioned landings. Since they hadn't yet finished the backcountry trails and Gage wasn't here for back up, Cam would have to pass on the temptation to take off for hours through the trails. He pushed off on his skis and headed through the trees to reach the more advanced downhill slopes.

As the day passed, it was fairly uneventful. Two teen boys overestimated their skiing prowess and tumbled together down one of the advanced slopes. Being teen boys, they insisted they were unharmed, but they respected Cam's insistence they wait for Don to ride up and bring them down on the snowmobile. He was relieved they'd managed to escape injury and wasn't about to let them try to ski the rest of the slope. Aside from that, he skied his way through the day, his eyes watchful on the other skiers.

He was coming to learn time did ease the loss of Eric. For so many months in Utah after the accident, Cam tried to ski and couldn't keep Eric out of his mind. He'd worried he'd never be able to enjoy skiing as much as he once had. It was that which prodded him to look for jobs elsewhere. Last Frontier Lodge was proving to offer what he needed— a chance to stay busy and focused with work, lots of time to ski, and a setting where Eric had never been, so Cam wasn't constantly bombarded with memories of Eric. He hadn't thought much of it when they'd been growing up together, but sharing so much of his life with Eric made it hard to escape the memories. He still struggled with guilt. Yet, he found it had been over a week since he last recalled replaying the accident in his mind.

Today, he found himself thinking mostly of Ginger. Last night was just...well, it was out of this world, and he was half out of his mind because of it. He hadn't even noticed a woman in over a year. Eric died and his world went into a skid. He thought he was managing to piece things back together, but he wasn't sure he was ready to consider a rela-tionship. The attraction between them burned so hot and fast, he couldn't ignore it, but he had no idea what Ginger was looking for. He mentally shook himself. It didn't help to get worked up over this. Maybe the heat between them would start to cool.

* * *

GINGER WOUND her scarf around her neck and walked through the automated door at the hospital. The cold slammed into her, and she paused in front of the building. She breathed in the icy air scented with snow and spruce. Marley and little Holly were sound asleep in the hospital room with Gage nodding off in the chair by the windows when Ginger left. Marley had asked her months ago to be with her for the delivery. Aside from Gage and Ginger, only Marley's parents, Holly and Stan, had been at the hospital. Marley's younger sister, Lacey, was out in the wilderness of the Arctic National Wildlife Refuge running a guided trip for a group. Trips like that were planned as far as a year in advance, and Lacey had been unable to find someone to take her place once Marley became pregnant. Ginger marveled that she'd been here most of the day. It felt as if almost no time had passed.

Her heart squeezed in her chest when she recalled the look on Marley's face when the nurse put Holly in her arms. She took another bracing breath of air and looked out over the view. The hospital was situated almost in the center of town on a small rise, which afforded a view of downtown Diamond Creek and Kachemak Bay. The bay glimmered under the colors of the setting sun. The sun was slipping behind the mountains on the far shore of the bay, leaving streaks of pink and lavender in its wake.

It felt like forever ago when she'd said goodbye to Cam this morning. Last night felt like a mirage—out of place, out of time. Simply thinking of him sent her pulse up a notch. She flushed with heat inside when she recalled the feel of him surging inside of her. When she'd woken beside him this morning and his amber eyes landed on her, she'd instantly wanted him again. If her phone hadn't rang when it did, she likely would have tackled him.

She started walking slowly across the parking lot and considered whether to call Cam. The wish to see him made her feel restless and vulnerable, so she tried to swat the feelings away. Her mind was having none of it. She hadn't been thinking much last night because Cam seemed to have this unique ability to turn her brain off. All she'd known was she couldn't turn away from the flames of desire flickering between them. She had no idea what to do with what was happening inside of her—her longing for Cam was a combustible mix of chemistry and emotion. It scared the hell out of her because nothing she'd experienced before compared, and she'd still been too vulnerable.

The snow crunched under her boots as she walked to her car. She suddenly realized if her car was here, that meant Cam had replaced her battery and brought her car over to the hospital. He'd parked it exactly where she'd parked his truck this morning. Her heart gave another kick. On top of everything, he happened to be kind and helpful, which made it that much harder to dismiss him. She climbed in her car and started it. She called Cam to thank him, experiencing a twinge of disappointment when all she got was his voice mail. She quickly thanked him for taking care of her car. Even though a suddenly loud voice inside of her really, really wanted to invite him over again, she forced herself to ignore that voice. She was too betwixt and between. Last night had blown the doors guarding her heart wide open. Without even trying, Cam had made her forget all of her promises to herself that had seemed so deceptively easy to keep for the last two years. The desire pounding between them made her forget everything. All she'd wanted was to be as close as physically possible to him. To make matters worse, he had to go and be downright amazing in bed. Before her marriage to Tony, she hadn't had a ton of experience. She'd dated here and there in high school and college, but sex had been pretty ho-hum. With Tony, it had been more of the same.

Then, there was last night. With Cam's mouth on her sex and his fingers stroking into her channel, she'd all but exploded with the force of her orgasm. Then, he'd slid inside of her and sent her flying again. She shook her head sharply. She couldn't keep this up. She was getting hot and bothered just sitting all by herself in the hospital parking lot. Even worse, she couldn't help but wonder what Cam thought. Given his life before he came to Diamond Creek, she imagined he'd had his fill of women traveling on the competitive ski circuit. Casual hook-ups were probably all in a day's work for him. *Yeah, but he doesn't seem like that kind of guy. At all. Right. A man as drop-dead gorgeous as him doesn't just ignore the opportunities thrown in his path.* She shook her head again. Silly internal arguments didn't help her. She didn't know what Cam wanted, or what he thought about last night, so speculation didn't do a damn thing but make her half-crazy inside.

But you know he's not a jerk. Oh, shut up! This soft side of herself, the side she thought she'd effectively squashed, couldn't help but try to have its say. The not-so-soft side was well versed in screeching loudly enough to be heard over all other thoughts. She couldn't help but laugh at herself. She put her car in gear and slowly drove away. She would go home and remember how much she loved life as a single woman. All these confusing feelings and uncertainties about Cam were precisely why she'd made the decision to forgo romance. Too much drama and potential for heartbreak.

When she arrived at home a short drive later, she stood in the living room and looked around. Cam must have tidied up before he left. The pullout sofa bed had been folded back into its side of the sectional. The sheets and blankets they'd used were neatly folded and left on the corner of the couch. Her eyes scanned the room, tracking over the candles that had lit the room up in a soft glow last night. She flushed recalling how Cam had looked in that shadowed light—his etched muscles and golden skin. Oh God. She had to get a grip.

George bounced down the spiral staircase and came to her feet. She leaned over and lifted him into her arms. She kicked her boots off and dropped her purse on the small table by the door before making her way into the kitchen. She quickly fed George and heated up leftovers from the pasta and sauce she'd shared with Cam the night before.

Her heart squeezed a little when she noticed Cam had followed her instructions for feeding George. George's two bowls for veggies and pellets were empty on the floor in the pantry.

She shoved Cam out of her thoughts and stomped into the living room to start a fire. She loved evenings beside her soapstone woodstove with food and a good show on for entertainment. After she had the fire started, she plunked down on the couch and turned on the television with a glass of wine in one hand and food in the other. George joined her after he finished nibbling on his dinner. No matter how hard she tried to remind herself she loved her life as it was, her thoughts kept wandering to Cam. Even if she tried to forget the sex, she couldn't forget how much she enjoyed being with him and how much fun she'd had playing cards last night. With a sigh, she eventually turned off the television, put her empty bowl and glass in the dishwasher and made her way upstairs to her bedroom. She fell asleep in her bed, trying and failing to forget how it felt to be snuggled up against Cam's warm body.

CHAPTER 10

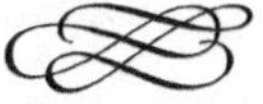

"Watch out!"

Cam heard the muffled shout from Don and took a step back just in the nick of time when a heavy spruce bough came tumbling loose from the tree. He grabbed it and tossed it out of the way. He and Don had been working most of the day up on the backcountry trails, cutting back trees and ensuring a wide enough trail for skiers to safely navigate.

He brushed away the snow the branch had dumped on him and turned to glance at Don. Don was leaning against his snowmobile. He grinned as he called out again. "That one must've been loose before you started cutting."

Cam leaned over and dragged the other branches he'd cut out of the way, tossing them onto the large sled attached to the back of his snowmobile. It was more of a giant cart on skids than a sled. Don also had one attached to the back of his snowmobile. To keep the area clear, they were hauling the brush back down the mountain to be used for a brush-fire at some point.

He paused for a moment and slowly turned in a circle.

They were on the last stretch of the marked trails. Seeing they'd loaded all the loose debris, he tugged his work gloves off and walked over to Don. "Looks like we're done here. How about we head over to the warming hut by where the trails start and pick up the pile we left there?"

Don nodded and pushed away from where he'd been leaning on the snowmobile. "Sure thing." He pulled a pair of gloves on and adjusted the visor on his hat before glancing back to Cam. "Did Gage happen to mention when he wanted to open these trails up for use?"

Cam shook his head. "Nope. I meant to ask you the same thing. After today, they're ready except for a run or two with the tracksetter to groom them, but we can have that done in a morning. Last time we talked about it, Gage wanted to get some signs up first though. Any ideas on that?"

Don shrugged. "Let's check with Delia when we get off the mountain. Marley usually handles that stuff, and if she talked to anyone about it, it would be Delia."

"Got it. Let's get going then." Cam walked back to his snowmobile, the snow crunching under his boots.

He climbed on and waited while Don started his snowmobile and slowly turned with the cart to head toward the warming hut. After several moments, Don was out of sight with the sound of his snowmobile engine fading. Cam sat quietly and looked around. It was a sunny day with the blue sky bright in contrast to the snow-covered landscape. He took a slow breath of the cool air. A raven called nearby with a magpie chattering in quick succession. Seconds later, the raven flew out of the trees with the magpie right behind it. Cam chuckled to himself as he watched the larger raven swoop and dodge to avoid the smaller and utterly fearless magpie. Sun glinted off the iridescent green and blue wings of the magpie and cast a colored shimmer on the snow below.

The familiar tight feeling in his chest wasn't there anymore. He was finally starting to see out the other side after Eric's death. Being outside on a snow-covered mountain had hurt for a while because it brought back too many memories. He'd worried he'd lose the peace he found outside, but it was coming back. Last Frontier Lodge was giving him what he needed to find room to breathe and heal. He looked ahead through a gap in the trees where a sliver of the bay was visible. The sun struck sparks on a glacier between the mountains on the far side of the bay. The glacier ice was mesmerizing—a deep, glowing blue. As many mountain ranges he'd visited, he'd never seen a glacier until he came to Alaska. He took another bracing breath of mountain air and started his snowmobile. Don would begin to wonder where he was if he was too far behind.

A few minutes later, he slowed his snowmobile and parked it beside Don's. With Don nowhere to be seen outside, Cam climbed off his snowmobile and pushed the door open to the small warming cabin. Don was standing by the heater, chugging water out of a water bottle. He took a last swallow and set the bottle down on a bench beside the heater.

"When you weren't right behind me, figured I'd warm up and take a break." Don removed his baseball cap and the thin fleece hat underneath it before sitting down on the bench and stretching his legs out. "Gotta say, I'm damn glad to have your help. I'm not as young as I used to be. Without you, the clearing work we did today would have to wait for Gage. I can help, but me trying to do it alone would be slow going."

Cam sat down across from Don on another bench. The warming cabins were small and basic. Each contained a propane heater, benches lining the walls and a cabinet with first aid supplies, water, and an emergency radio. Cam slipped his gloves off and removed his hat as well. Don snagged another bottle of water from the cabinet to his side and tossed it to Cam. After several gulps, Cam sighed and looked back toward Don. "You keep saying you're not as young as you used to be, but you set a hell of a pace. I can't imagine how hard you worked when you were younger," he said with a shake of his head.

Don chuckled and paused to empty his bottle of water. "I can work fast, but the heavy work is what I need help with. Like what you did today—all that cutting overhead and dragging the heavier limbs—not for me anymore. Enjoy your back while you can."

Cam grinned. "My back does okay, but I've been pretty hard on my body. Competitive skiing isn't as rough as some sports, but backcountry skiing comes with its share of falls. All in all, I've been lucky, but I've gotten pretty banged up a few times."

Don nodded. He was quiet for a moment. "How long has it been since you raced?"

Cam's stomach knotted. For a split second, he started to feel that panicky feeling—the feeling that came whenever something reminded him of Eric. He forced himself to breathe and remember he needed to learn to talk about Eric. He met Don's kind, steady gaze. "Not since my brother died. It's been, uh, well it's been hard to think about competing again."

Don nodded slowly, but he remained quiet as if he was waiting for more. Don was an easy man to be with, the kind of man who made you feel as if he understood. Cam figured he probably did. He'd lost his wife to cancer earlier than most, so he wasn't a stranger to loss.

Cam found himself talking in a way he hadn't been able to talk about Eric yet. With his family, it was hard because he was hypersensitive to how Eric's death had affected them. With Don, there was none of that worry. "Honestly, I hadn't planned to compete much longer. I'm only two years away from forty. I didn't quit because Eric died. It was more like I finalized a decision I'd been thinking about. My family needed me, and I needed to slow down. I won't ever stop skiing, but I don't miss the constant travel and everything else that goes with the competition circuit."

Don nodded slowly. "What brought you to Last Frontier Lodge?"

"I love to ski and I enjoy ski instruction. I'd bounced around at a few jobs before I saw the ad for this one. Of all the places there are to ski, I'd never been to Alaska, so I figured it would be a good place to regroup."

"Any idea how long you'll be around?"

Cam shrugged. "Before I came up here, I had no idea one way or the other. Now that I'm here, I love it. Last Frontier Lodge is a great ski lodge, and Gage couldn't be easier to work for. Diamond Creek's a great little town too. At the moment, I'm not planning on leaving anytime soon."

Another slow nod from Don before his eyes narrowed. "Hope you don't mind me saying anything, but you might as well hear it from me than someone else. I get the sense there might be something between you and Ginger. None of my business really, but I tend to stick my nose wherever I choose," he said with a chuckle and a shrug. "I've known her since she was a girl, and she has a heart of gold. She went through the wringer with her divorce, so, uh, you might find she has some pretty protective friends."

Questions flew through Cam's mind, but he wasn't about to grill Don. He experienced a twinge of anger toward the faceless ex who put her through the wringer, as Don phrased it. On the heels of that, a fierce sense of protectiveness rose within him. He didn't like knowing she'd been hurt. He considered that he'd unintentionally stumbled into the small town rumor mill. It wasn't that he wanted to hide anything, but he was befuddled by his feelings for Ginger. The attraction was like a brush fire gone wild, and his feelings were tangled up in it. His heart had a soft spot he hadn't known existed—just for Ginger. He glanced back up at Don who was waiting patiently. "I suppose you might be one of those protective friends, huh?"

Don grinned unabashedly. "You got it. I'm not gonna get all bossy with you. Nothing like that. Just thought you'd want to know things were ugly in her divorce and, far as I know, she hasn't dated anyone since. If my hunch is on target with you two, make sure you treat her right. Don't make any promises you can't keep. That's all I'm saying."

The idea of making promises of the romantic kind to anyone hadn't crossed Cam's mind. He was still trying to adjust to the nerve-rattling and heart-shaking attraction he had to Ginger. Don was about ten steps ahead of him. He realized Don was waiting again, so he took a breath and gathered his thoughts. "Look, you're obviously pretty damn observant. I won't pretend I'm not interested in Ginger, but you can rest assured I won't make any promises I can't keep."

Don nodded firmly and stood. "Good enough. Ginger's pretty independent, so it's not like I'd expect you to make some kind of commitment. Whatever happens, make sure it's on the up and up. That's all."

Cam tried to ignore the odd way his heart clenched when he considered that whatever happened with Ginger's divorce sounded like it had done a number on her. He met Don's eyes and stood. "No worries. I know you haven't known me long, but I don't play games, so you don't need to worry I'll be anything other than honest."

Don swiped his hats off the bench, putting the thin fleece hat on and the baseball cap over it. "Hope you understand why I said something."

Cam's heart tightened again, but this time it wasn't because of Ginger. One of the characteristics he'd come to appreciate about Diamond Creek was how tight-knit the community was. He could see the flipside to that would be sometimes people might come across as nosy. Don didn't come across that way. It was clear he cared about Ginger. "I understand," Cam replied.

At that, they walked outside, each pulling their gloves on. In the crisp air with the sun starting to set, they quickly loaded up the pile of branches they'd left by the cabin. Cam followed Don slowly down the slope, keeping to the far side and clear of skiers. After they unloaded the carts and put the snowmobiles away in the garage, they headed inside. The staff entrance led to a hallway directly off the restaurant kitchen. The aromas of fresh-baked bread mingling with whatever variety of meals Delia had on the menu for the evening wafted into the hallway. After peeling off his outerwear gear, Cam raced up the back stairs to his suite for a quick shower. He and Don had worked solid all day, so he'd worked up quite a sweat. He needed to wash the day off before dinner.

* * *

GINGER KICKED her boots on the threshold, knocking the snow loose as she stepped into the lodge. She threaded her way through the cluster of people waiting for tables. Harry Lawson, the supervisor for the floor staff at the restaurant and Delia's right-hand, gave her a quick wave. "Gage had me hold the usual table, although he and Marley won't be down tonight."

Ginger paused by the small desk where he was managing a waitlist for tables. "Have you seen them at all today?"

Harry flashed a grin. "Of course! Marley brought Holly down to show her off after the first night back. I know you've seen her plenty, so you know how adorable she is."

Ginger laughed. "Oh yeah. She's about the cutest baby

ever. I'm glad they're taking some time to themselves though. I bet it's been a merry-go-round with visitors."

Harry shrugged. "I call it the baby craze. Whenever someone has a new baby, everyone flips out until they get used to it."

A couple stepped to the desk. Ginger gave a wave and left Harry to work. Though Harry worked at a ski lodge in Alaska, he was far from an outdoorsy person. He prided himself on only skiing the bunny slopes and was heavily involved in the arts community in Diamond Creek. Delia had lured him away from another successful restaurant in Diamond Creek with the promise of year-round work. Many businesses in Diamond Creek were only open seasonally when the tourists flocked to Alaska during the spring, summer and fall months. Since Gage had reopened Last Frontier Lodge, it had brought back a flood of travelers to Diamond Creek during the winter months. Gage had also coordinated with a few local businesses to keep the lodge open in the summer for tourists seeking wilderness experiences, such as chartered fishing, flightseeing and other summer activities.

Ginger glanced around the restaurant. It was completely full, which was the case most nights. She felt a hum of pride for Delia. Delia had been so nervous when Gage offered her the job of managing the restaurant, reception and house-keeping staff. Not only had the job landed her in the path of Garrett Hamilton when he came for a visit and fell head over heels in love with her, but it had given her the financial stability and peace of mind she so needed being a single mother. Delia had done a fabulous job of making the lodge restaurant a local and tourist favorite in town.

Ginger's eyes landed on the booth in the back corner of the restaurant, the one closest to the kitchen and the one Gage kept reserved for family and friends most nights. The moment her eyes coasted across Cam, her pulse rocketed.

Oh. My. God. You have got a serious thing for him. If you were hoping it wouldn't be obvious to the whole free world, you'd better get a grip and fast. Somehow, she'd gotten through the last two days without calling him even though she thought about it multiple times a day. The first day she'd been so preoccupied with Marley having a baby, she'd only thought of Cam in free moments and then when she went home. Day two hadn't been so easy. Dear God. She was counting the days since he'd set her body on fire and shown her how weak the walls around her heart really were. *This is not good. Not good at all.* Meanwhile, he was front and center any time she showed up at the lodge and had been easily absorbed into her circle of friends, so it was pretty much impossible for her to avoid him.

Cam sat on one side of the booth with an elbow resting on the table while he gestured with his hand as he talked to Delia and Garrett. His amber hair glinted under the soft lights in the restaurant. Don pushed through the swinging door from the kitchen and snagged a chair nearby, angling it beside the booth. She gulped in air and tried to calm her racing pulse, but it appeared to have a mind of its own. She put one foot in front of the other and kept walking. When she reached the booth, Don glanced up and immediately gestured to the empty spot in the booth beside Cam. "Joining us?" he asked.

Ginger managed to nod, but she couldn't seem to form words. Yet again, Cam's mere presence stole her capacity to speak. She focused on hanging her jacket on the corner of the booth and fumbling with nothing in her purse as she sat down. When she looked up, she forced herself to look only in Delia and Garrett's direction first. She didn't need to try to look at Cam and have her body run wild.

"Hey!" she said brightly. "I love it when you give yourself enough time to eat," she said to Delia, trying to talk about anything to keep her mind off of Cam.

Delia smiled. "I always give myself time to eat."

Garrett's arm was draped across the back of the booth. He squeezed his hand on Delia's shoulder. "You usually eat on your feet. Pretty sure Ginger's point was its nice when you take time to relax and eat with us."

Delia rolled her eyes. "Okay, okay. I try, but it's always so busy."

Garrett dipped his head and dropped a lingering kiss on the side of Delia's neck. "Exactly, so what does it matter if you take a break?" he asked when he lifted his head again.

Delia flushed and grabbed her water for a gulp. She focused her warm blue eyes on Ginger. "How's it going?"

Ginger shrugged. "Nothing new for me. I was worn out yesterday after being at the hospital for the delivery. I've decided if it's that much work to be there, labor must be way worse."

Delia nodded emphatically. "I can vouch for that."

The waitress arrived to take her order. In need of something to take the edge off, Ginger ordered a glass of red wine in addition to her meal. By the time the waitress walked away, Don and Garrett were discussing something. Ginger tried to take a fortifying breath before she looked at Cam, but her lungs weren't working so well. Without even looking his way, she could feel the heat of Cam's body near hers. He emanated heat, like a slow burn furnace.

The moment she turned her head, his eyes snagged hers. His eyes coasted over her face like a caress, the warm amber of his gaze sending slivers of heat shooting through her. He arched a brow, his mouth curling up at one corner. "Hey there." His words were low enough, she felt as if they were for her alone to hear. While his greeting was benign, her body reacted as if he'd whispered something naughty to her. She must have been silent a beat too long because he arched a brow.

Say something, you fool!

"Hey, uh, how's it going?" she asked, her words coming out stilted. By this point, she wasn't blushing just because he was near, but because she felt like a bumbling idiot.

"Pretty good. Don and I've been working our butts off the last two days. We have the new backcountry trails course ready to go. Just need to find out what signs Gage wants up there." Cam turned to Delia. "Hey Delia, your dad thought maybe you'd know the plans for signs up on the trails. Any ideas?"

Delia, Don and Garrett turned their way. Ginger schooled her expression to neutral and prayed her blush had faded, or the light was too dim for them to notice. Meanwhile, her pulse galloped along, unperturbed by the inconvenience of her practically melting into a puddle at simply sitting beside Cam.

Don fiddled with a toothpick and gestured to Cam. "We've got those trails ready for the green light. It'd be nice to surprise Gage and open the course up sooner, but we both know he wanted some signs. Marley usually helps out with that stuff, so I thought maybe she talked to you," he said with a nod in Delia's direction.

"Marley planned ahead," Delia said with a grin. "She figured you guys would finish up soon, so she had Risa at Midnight Sun Arts paint some signs. I can give Risa a call tomorrow and see if they're ready."

"Wow, Gage isn't messing around about bringing this place up a notch. Marley mentioned to me he was gradually replacing the old signage outside and in the lodge with more artsy stuff," Ginger said, feeling relieved to have something to focus on other than Cam.

"He's on a roll," Garrett said with a chuckle. "Gotta give it to him. When he told us he was moving here to revamp this place, I had no idea how well it would go. Of course, it helps to have the best chef in town running the restaurant." Garrett dipped his head for a kiss on Delia's cheek.

Ginger felt a curl of longing around her heart. While she'd been so happy to watch Marley and Delia find love, not for a minute had she experienced any hopes for herself. Until Cam. He was stirring deep waters, waters she'd hoped to leave undisturbed. She couldn't turn back the tide, but she was still struggling to adjust to her feelings and was nowhere near feeling comfortable enough to hope for something more. Yet, her hopeful little heart, the one she'd been so successful at keeping quiet, kept chirping in her ear.

Delia flushed again and rolled her eyes. "I'm happy the restaurant's doing so well, but Gage and Marley have really put the work in at every level. The trail signs are just more on top of everything else." Her eyes bounced between Cam and Don. "Anyway, signs are on deck. I'll call tomorrow."

Don and Cam grinned simultaneously leading Delia to burst out laughing. "You guys are damn proud of yourselves, huh?"

Don shrugged sheepishly. "Hey, Cam put the hard work in. It's not easy to be a step ahead of Gage, so it'd be nice to surprise him."

Conversation moved along with occasional visitors pausing at the table, including Becky Wright, the teacher from work who'd been gossiping about how sexy Cam was. While Ginger wholeheartedly agreed with Becky, she wasn't particularly comfortable having Becky notice she was socializing with him. She loved her hometown, but sometimes it felt like living in a fish bowl. Everyone could see too much too easily.

Becky was with her husband and son, so she managed only a coy wave, but Ginger mentally reminded herself to be prepared for Becky's questions about Cam the next time she encountered her at work. After a slow dinner, the small group started to break up. Don left early as usual. Garrett left to pick up Nick, Delia's seven-year old son, from his school basketball practice. That left Ginger at the booth with Cam and Delia.

Cam excused himself for a bathroom break. Delia leaned her elbows on the table and looked Ginger square in the eye. "So when were you planning to mention this thing with Cam?"

Ginger's cheeks were hot as she stared back at Delia. She tried to play it cool. "What are you talking about?"

Delia leaned back and crossed her arms. "Don't play that game with me. I'm not blind. You two are trying your damnedest not to look at each other, but when you do, I'm afraid I might have to call the fire department."

Ginger put her face in her hands and groaned. "Oh God. Is it that obvious?" When she lifted her head and brushed her hair back, Delia nodded emphatically. Beyond being plain embarrassed, Ginger felt so exposed. She'd been so confident she'd never fall for anyone again that she was shaken.

"Okay, maybe there's kind of a thing. Could we talk about it later though?" She gestured across the restaurant to Cam who was returning from the restroom. She watched as women's eyes all over the restaurant tracked him, some surreptitiously, others blatantly. She sighed again. "Tell me why I had to go and have this...whatever...for some guy who has all the women drooling over him. It's not ideal."

Delia laughed softly. "You owe me coffee, so we can talk. In the meantime, who cares if other women drool over him? He doesn't even pay attention. Except to you. And don't even start with how you look. You're one of the smartest women I know and beautiful on top of it."

Ginger's defensiveness eased. She had good friends, and Delia was one of the best. She was one hundred percent there for her friends whenever they needed her. Right now, even if Ginger didn't like it, she needed her friends. "Okay, this ends now. We'll talk later." She kept her eyes trained on

Delia when Cam got within earshot. "How late are you working tonight?" she asked, putting the conversation firmly back onto the mundane.

Delia lifted a shoulder. "Until the kitchen closes for orders, which means ten o'clock."

As Cam slid into the booth beside Ginger, this time hemming her in on the inside of the bench seat, Delia glanced at her watch. "Speaking of work, I should get back in the kitchen. I need to take care of some pastry prep work for tomorrow morning." At that, she slipped out from across the booth and stood. She looked to Cam. "After I talk to Risa, I'll let you and my dad know. The signs might be ready to go."

"Thanks for checking on those. I'm sure I'll see you tomorrow," Cam replied with a smile.

Delia nodded, her eyes bouncing to Ginger. "G'night," she said with a small wave before she hurried off.

It was just Ginger and Cam now. Ginger was close to melting and flustered by the almost overwhelming pull she felt for him. The pulse of desire between them had ebbed and flowed during dinner with conversation and the presence of others to distract her. Yet, here with him alone, the desire had a life force of its own. Heat swirled in her center, radiating outward through her entire body. She could feel the moisture between her thighs and clenched her legs together, as if she could will it away. That had the unfortunate effect of heightening her awareness, the subtle pressure sending streaks of pleasure through her. Her breath was shallow when she looked to her side.

Cam's eyes were right there, as if he'd been waiting for her. They sat for several long moments, eyes locked to each other. Finally, she tore hers away and took a gulp of air. She felt his palm slide onto her thigh, so strong and warm. She wasn't sure what he intended, but her body went haywire. She literally had to fight to hold still. She felt raw, exposed and filled with need. Unable to tolerate thinking of it in any other way, she focused solely on the physical desire. She wanted Cam like she'd never wanted any man, and he took her to places she'd never been. There was nothing wrong with exploring more of that.

She took another gulp of air and looked his way again. His eyes immediately lifted from the table to hers. His thumb stroked in a slow arc on her thigh, each stroke sending a throb through her channel. He cleared his throat. "I meant to call you if I didn't see you tonight," he said, his words low and taut.

She swallowed and nodded, shifting her hips restlessly. She hadn't meant to, but her unconscious move nudged his hand higher up on her thigh, his thumb landing in the crease of her hip. He was so, so close to where she needed him. She was in serious trouble. She was sitting in the restaurant where half the town could see them, and all she could think about was having his magical fingers inside of her. She was seriously contemplating how they could manage this in the restaurant, including the logistics of how she could give him just as much pleasure as he could give her. In public. The table did conveniently mask the fact his hand was inches away from the center of her desire.

She took a deep breath in a futile effort to clear her mind. "I need you," she blurted out.

When he arched a brow and started to speak, she cut him off. "Now. Let's go to your suite."

Cam was completely still for a moment before he nodded his head sharply. "Right. Okay."

His hand left her thigh as he stood from the table. She felt the absence of his touch immediately. She grabbed her purse and quickly stood up. She started to walk briskly out of the restaurant. She knew they could go up the back stairs to his suite, but she didn't want it to be obvious to anyone where they were going. Cam caught up to her when she'd almost reached the archway leading into the reception area. "You forgot your jacket," he said.

She glanced over and saw her puffy red down jacket hooked over his arm. "Thanks for getting it."

She started to reach for it as they walked past Harry at the reception desk. "I got it," Cam said softly. He nodded in Harry's direction. "Night, Harry. You in tomorrow morning?"

"Nope. I'm not on duty until evening again. See you then. Night, Ginger," Harry replied with a wave.

She returned the wave and breathed a sigh of relief when they passed through the reception area into the expansive hallway and saw no one around. She paused and looked up at Cam. His amber eyes coasted over her. She practically felt the burn of his gaze. He turned and slipped his hand down her spine where it came to rest in the dip of her waist. His touch sent a jolt of electricity through her. She hurried at his side up the main stairs and through the halls, so focused on getting alone in a room with him that she didn't even care if anyone saw them.

They reached a door at the far end of one of the hallways. Cam swiped his key card in the lock and shouldered through the entrance. As soon as they stepped inside the room, he kicked the door shut behind them and whirled her around. Her purse fell off her shoulder and onto the floor. He tossed her jacket behind him and planted both palms on the door behind her. His eyes were dark and intent. Without a word, his lips crashed to hers.

CHAPTER 11

The last thing Cam saw as he nearly lunged at Ginger was the flash of blue fire in her eyes. Somehow, he had no idea how really, he managed to keep his hands to himself and behave like a rational man in front of everyone during dinner. Underneath his attempt to be casual and social had been the constant drumbeat of lust pounding through his body. Ginger was like a drug for his body. Kissing her was like breaking the surface of water after being underneath far too long. He fit his mouth over hers and poured his need into their kiss. She arched up into him, her tongue stroking against his. Her lips were so soft and her mouth so sweet that it only drove him wilder. He'd been rock-hard for hours. Kissing her was a relief, but it also sent his need for her into overdrive.

He tore his lips from hers, frantic to taste more of her. He traced his tongue along her throat, savoring the moans humming through her. She tasted like she smelled—like strawberries and vanilla. She wore a fitted blouse, her full breasts straining at the buttons. He was too driven to care when he yanked at the blouse and a button went flying, pinging against the wall before it clattered on the floor. Ginger sighed deeply when he peeled her blouse apart and flicked his thumb under the clasp of her bra. He was too impatient to take it slow right now and needed to feel the tight beads of her nipples in his mouth.

Without preamble, he leaned forward and stroked his tongue in a swirl around one nipple before he sucked it swiftly. At her cry, he bit down softly and smiled against her skin when his name came out with a sharp gasp. He almost came in his jeans when she arched her back, pressing into his mouth when he gave the same attention to her other breast. He forced himself to take a step back. He thought he could somehow get control of himself, but he took one look at her and his knees nearly buckled.

She leaned against the door with her shirt open to her waist. Her nipples glistened in the dim light from the single lamp he'd left on in the corner. Her breath was heaving. Her blue eyes were wild—flashing with fire. Her dark hair fell in loose waves around her shoulders, mussed and rumpled. She reached out with one hand and hooked it under the hem of his shirt. With a single finger, she lifted his shirt up slowly, her eyes on him. She stroked her other palm up his chest. His heart hammered inside his chest. With another stroke, she moved down and cupped his cock in her palm, sliding back and forth over the denim of his jeans. Barely able to see through the haze of lust, he grabbed his shirt at the back of his neck and yanked it off in a single swoop. He dug his wallet out of his pocket and nearly dropped it in his haste to get a condom out. After the other night, he'd made a quick trip to the drugstore to make sure he was prepared if he was lucky enough to have another night with Ginger.

Meanwhile, Ginger was swiftly unbuttoning his jeans. He stepped closer and nudged her chin up for another kiss. Her lips were so damn soft. It was like coming home to a home he'd never known he had. Several sense-stealing moments later, he lifted his head and dragged his hand down her side, cupping the edge of her breast, before stroking his palm between her thighs. She wore a pair of soft, swingy pants that hugged her hips. The cotton was thin enough he could feel the damp heat of her through it. Her breath hitched when he stroked a finger back and forth.

He couldn't wait anymore and shoved her pants down, her underwear along with them. She kicked them off, along with the clogs she wore. She was quite the multi-tasker, somehow freeing his cock in the midst of this. His jeans hung low on his hips while she curled her fist around him and stroked. He couldn't hold back his groan. Her hand on his cock felt so damn good. She shimmied down against the door, her lips trailing a path of fire down his chest and abdomen. Kneeling, she tilted her head up and caught his eyes before she dragged her tongue along his cock. With his heart pounding so hard he thought he might break a rib, she took him in her mouth. The hot, wet heat of her mouth nearly pushed him beyond his endurance. She alternated with bringing him fully into her mouth, licking, sucking and stroking. The pressure built and built within him until he was pushed against the edge of his release.

He barely managed to choke out her name and reached down to pull her up. She leaned against the door, her lips swollen and her eyes hazy. He tore the condom out of its packet. His eyes on her, he rolled it on and hooked his hand under her knee. Lifting it high, he stepped into the cradle of her hips. He lifted her against him, using the door behind her for support. Her eyes widened when he dragged his cock back and forth through her folds. She was so wet, the moisture of her soaked his fingers. His cock throbbed as he tried to force himself to hold back. Her head slammed back against the door.

"Cam! Now!"

He looked into her eyes, wild with need and a tinge of

frustration. He surged into her in one swift stroke, seating himself to the hilt. Her head fell forward, landing on his shoulder, as she groaned. She felt so damn good—slick, tight and hot. He held still for enough time to gather some control and then began to move. She curled her legs around him and flexed with every stroke, bringing him deeper and deeper.

With her soft pants and cries raining down around him, the pressure inside unraveled and he pounded into her. He could hear the door rattle with each drive, but Ginger thrashed against him. He couldn't slow down if he tried. He felt as if he was barreling toward his own unraveling—every stroke into her wet velvet clench pushed him further and further. When he felt her channel being to throb around him, he dragged his thumb down between them, circling over the slick nub where they were joined. She went taut and cried out hoarsely. Only then did he let go into the hot rush. Several deep strokes and his own release rocked him, so intense that he had to brace a hand against the door behind her to hold himself up.

THE SOUND of a raven calling outside the window woke Ginger. She was sleeping curled up on her side with Cam spooned behind her. His warm, muscled form felt so good, she sighed and closed her eyes. After he'd blown her mind again last night, she'd somehow pulled herself together and started to get ready to go home. Cam had tugged her to him and attempted to persuade her to stay there, but when she'd reminded him she had to get home to take care of George, next thing she knew he was following her back to her place. Falling asleep tangled up with him was a luxury she wasn't so sure she could allow herself too many times. It felt so good to be held against his strong body—a physical and emotional comfort she wanted to sink into and savor.

Her bed was built in against the windows. Whoever originally built the home clearly wanted to capitalize on the phenomenal view. She'd worried the windows would be too cold in the winter, but they were double insulated and she'd hung quilted curtains over them. She'd come to love falling asleep with a view of the moon and stars and the sunrise to greet her when she woke. She nudged the curtain out of the way and looked out over the bay. The winter dawn was slowly coming. The sky above the mountains was barely light with wisps of lavender and pink reaching skyward. The sun had yet to make its appearance. She let the curtain fall and slowly rotated in Cam's embrace. No matter how much she wanted to laze around in bed this morning, she knew he needed to get back to the lodge before his absence became too obvious. It wasn't that he couldn't have a life outside of the lodge, but rather that Ginger preferred not to broadcast his night with her just yet.

The steady rhythm of Cam's breath was interrupted when she rolled over to face him. His palm slid from where it had been resting on her hip to her low belly. He shifted his legs and straightened them. She felt the shivering stretch of his body in her core. His eyes opened in the dim light of her bedroom. In the soft quiet, they lay still. After several moments, he cleared his throat. "S'pose I should get up and get going."

She lifted her hand and traced it along his collarbone. "You should. What time do you need to get back to the lodge?"

"I'm usually up and at it before sunrise. Of course, sunrise around here is pretty late in the winter," he said with a gruff chuckle.

She kept tracing her fingertip back and forth along his collarbone. A wash of emotion crested inside of her. The wish to stay right here with him was an unfamiliar feeling. She simultaneously wanted to dive into it and run from it. Internally restless, she needed something to do. "How about I make some coffee before you go?" she asked as she kicked the covers free of her legs and sat up.

Cam pushed himself up on his elbows causing the sheet to fall to his waist. Her mouth went dry. Dear God, the man was just too damn sexy for his own good. His chest and abs were practically carved from stone. She swallowed and tried to slow her pulse, which had taken off at a gallop the moment he sat up.

"Coffee would be great."

"Got it," she said quickly as she scrambled past him on the bed.

The hardwood floor was cool under her feet. She scurried to the bathroom just off her bedroom, threw on her warm, fleece robe and stuffed her feet in slippers. She paused when she stepped back into the bedroom and flicked on a small lamp on a table beside the bathroom door. Her bedroom contained the built in bed by the windows, which was piled high with pillows and a fluffy down quilt. Aside from the bed, there were nightstands on either side of the bed, a dresser on the wall across from the bathroom and a large, comfy chair by the closet, which she tended to use as an improvised laundry basket. At the moment, clothes were draped all over it.

A multi-colored circular rug was on the floor at the foot of the bed. Cam had leaned over to peer through the curtains. "Wow, you can't beat this view for watching the sunrise."

She looked through the small gap between the curtains to see the sun cresting the mountains, its white-gold rays breaking through the colors. "I know. I love waking up here." When he glanced to her, she gestured to the bathroom. "Feel free to use the shower. I'll go get some coffee started."

The temptation to crawl back in bed was so strong, she had to force her feet to move. Once she got through her bedroom door, she hurried down the spiral staircase. She turned up the thermostat and greeted George who leapt down from his favored morning windowsill and followed her into the kitchen. She started a pot of coffee and then fed George.

A while later, she looked through the living room windows and watched Cam drive away. Her heart squeezed in her chest. This morning was too easy, hence her mind was running in circles. He'd had a cup of coffee and waved off her offer to make breakfast, saying he needed to get back up to the lodge. The sound of his engine faded, and she turned to look out the back windows. The sun hadn't quite fully crested the mountains, but the sky was brightening and shimmers of light rippled on the surface of the water.

Her mind was a jumble of confusion. She'd so thoroughly convinced herself a relationship wasn't in the cards for her, she didn't quite know what to do with how she felt. Two nights with Cam and her hopeful heart was clamoring for her to pay attention. With a sigh, she ran upstairs and jumped in the shower.

CHAPTER 12

Cam leaned against the bar and grinned at the sight of Don gingerly cradling Marley and Gage's daughter, Holly. Babies were cute all by themselves, but put a baby in the arms of a man like Don—rough around the edges with a warm heart—and together they were beyond adorable. It was the quietest time of day at the lodge. Late afternoon was when the lunch rush was over and most of the guests were up on the mountain. The restaurant was close to empty. Gage and Marley had emerged from their private quarters in the lodge with Holly. Cam had returned from a busy morning working with Don to post all the trail signs Marley had ordered.

Delia had sent him down to Midnight Sun Arts early this morning to pick up the signs. Risa Thomas, the gallery manager, had met him at the door. Once upon a time, Cam might have been drawn to her with her dark hair and flashing brown eyes, but Ginger was all he could think about these days. He'd been relieved at his lack of attraction to Risa when her husband, the local chief of police, had arrived while they were loading the artistically rendered trail signs in the back of Cam's truck. Cam had enjoyed chatting with Darren and Risa for a few minutes before he raced back up to the lodge. The more time he spent in Diamond Creek, the more he liked it. Anytime he met someone new, they spent time asking about what brought him to the area and were warm and welcoming. He had enough sense to know, in a town this size, he was being assessed as well, but he didn't mind. Whether he'd expected it or not, Diamond Creek was starting to feel like a place he could call home.

He glanced around the room. Gage was seated on one of the bar stools, looking more tired than usual likely due to the monumental life change of having a newborn baby to help care for. Marley was beside Don, helping him adjust Holly's head in the crook of his elbow. Delia was busy wiping down tables while she reviewed the menu with Harry who walked alongside her jotting down notes in a small notepad he kept in his pocket at all times. Cam was coming to love the easy camaraderie here. Ivy's prodding about settling down somewhere rose in the back of his mind. He wasn't quite ready to think about that yet.

The phone behind the bar jangled. At the moment, no one was staffing the bar because there was no need. Harry strode away from Delia and snagged the phone as it rang a second time. After a pause, Harry quickly recited the hours for the restaurant and took a name for reservations before hanging up. He glanced to Gage who was seated at the far end of the bar, talking with Marley and Don. Harry took a few steps until he was across from Cam at the bar. "So, what's the word on the backcountry course? Is it a go for tomorrow?" he asked, his voice low.

Cam nodded. "All set. Don gave it the green light. You and Delia can have the front desk start letting guests know."

Harry grinned. "Good work. It's nearly impossible to

surprise Gage, so this'll be fun. Pretty sure he didn't think the course would be ready for another few weeks."

Cam chuckled. "I've noticed he's hard to surprise. He's a planner."

Harry stepped away. "That he is, but Delia said Marley didn't tell him about ordering the signs, so he still thinks he has to take care of that." Harry grinned as he headed for the kitchen.

A while later, Cam returned to his room and peeled off his clothes for a shower. Ginger had been dancing at the edges of his thoughts all day. It had taken all of his discipline to get up and leave her bed this morning. The only thing that drove him was his strong work ethic. He'd never in his life blown off work.

Whatever was happening with Ginger was unsettling. He couldn't stop thinking about her, which was a first for him. While he hadn't had time for serious relationships with his busy travel schedule, he'd dated here and there. No woman had ever gotten to him the way she did. He couldn't resist her, yet he worried things were moving too far, too fast.

He considered Don's comment about her divorce. He couldn't help but wonder about what happened. He'd meant it when he told Don he wouldn't make any false promises. The problem was he didn't know what he wanted, or what she wanted. Meanwhile, the attraction between them was a raging fire that couldn't be contained.

After he dried off and changed into a comfortable pair of sweatpants and a t-shirt, he decided he'd swing through the kitchen and bring a tray up to his room. He wasn't sure he was up for company tonight and definitely wasn't sure he was up for running into Ginger. To be more accurate, he desperately wanted to encounter her, but he had no idea how to contain his feelings to the point it rattled him.

After a quiet dinner with the news rumbling in the background, he snagged his phone off the coffee table by the couch and called Ivy. She picked up right away.

"I was just about to call you," Ivy announced by way of greeting. "I swear I think we have a telepathic connection."

Cam grinned. "Maybe so. How's it going?"

"Let's see, I studied, graded papers for a class I'm teaching and wrote another research paper today. That's basically my life everyday. How's life on the last frontier?"

Cam thought for a minute and realized the answer was...good. In the early months after Eric died, he'd worried he'd spend the rest of his life half-lying about how he was doing. His grief was still like a giant bruise on his heart, but its pain was easing bit by bit. Life wasn't perfect, but he could actually say things were pretty okay.

"Life on the last frontier is good."

"Really?" The hope in Ivy's voice squeezed his heart.

"Yes, Ivy. Things are good."

Ivy was quiet for a beat and then her next question flew out. "What's happening with that woman you mentioned?"

He didn't even bother to hold back his groan. "Really, Ivy? All I said was I thought she might be interesting. It's not like we're about to get married. I'm only committed for this ski season right now." Ivy's question bumped up against his own uncertainty. He hadn't thought beyond this winter and certainly hadn't considered anything even in the neighborhood of a relationship. He didn't need his wishful sister to pin her hopes on something he didn't even know if he wanted, much less if he was ready for.

"I know you're only there for this season right now, but that could change. You could use a place to call home. You're like a rolling stone."

He swallowed his sigh and leaned his head back on the couch. "I know you're worried. How about you let me enjoy the winter? I'm not so sure it's a great plan to be looking to put roots down this far away from Mom and Dad." While their parents were still keeping busy and showed no signs of slowing down, ever since Eric died, Cam worried about them and worried he needed to find a way to be closer.

Ivy didn't bother to hold back her elaborate sigh. "Mom and Dad will be fine no matter where you are. The flight isn't too long anyway. They've always said they don't plan to retire in Utah anyway. It'd be silly for you to plan your life around where they are now when that's probably not where they're going to be in the next five years or so."

"You've got a point, but ease up on the pressure, okay? I'm enjoying the work here, and Diamond Creek is beautiful. Did you get a chance to see when you might be able to come up for a visit?"

Ivy wisely let the topic drop about him settling down somewhere. "Oh right. I checked the semester calendar, and I have a few days free during the March break. I'm not sure if that will be the same time Mom and Dad get up there, but I'm coming either way."

"Perfect. Tell me when, and I'll book your flight."

"When are you going to stop trying to pay for everything for me?" she demanded.

"When you're not working and trying to finish your graduate degree at the same time. I fully expect you to support me in retirement as payback."

He could practically see her rolling her eyes. Ivy worked her tail off to keep her student loans as minimal as possible. Their parents did fine, but they weren't swimming in cash to cover all of Ivy's academic expenses. She was brilliant, so she got scholarships both at the undergraduate and graduate level, but those only covered tuition. He and Eric made pretty good money over the years they raced. They also had few expenses beyond travel, so he had plenty saved up.

Ivy finally laughed. "Fine. You can buy these tickets, but if you stay there, I'm buying the next trip."

"Deal. Now it's your turn. You've been on me about dating, so what's the scoop for you?"

"There is no scoop. I read, research, write and teach. There is no time in my schedule anywhere to meet anyone, much less to go on a date."

"You know, for someone who goes on and on about how important it is for me to find someone special, you've got all kinds of excuses for yourself."

"I know, but they're legitimate. I'm not avoiding, I'm seriously too busy."

"Fine. But when you're done with school, we'll be revisiting this topic unless you back off of me."

He hung up to the sound of Ivy's laugh.

* * *

GINGER DUCKED her head down as she walked quickly across the parking lot. Today was clear and bright with a bracing wind whipping off the bay. She was meeting Delia for lunch and coffee at Misty Mountain Café for the coffee date she'd promised her. She had two favorite coffee places, Misty Mountain and Red Truck Coffee, but only Misty Mountain was open in the winter. She appreciated that detail because it allowed her to be loyal to Misty Mountain in the winter and Red Truck Coffee in the summer. Another gust of wind blasted across the parking lot, and she broke into a jog. When she reached the door, a couple conveniently walked out and she slipped right past them into the toasty warm café.

She pushed her hood back and glanced around. When she didn't see Delia, she took a few steps to stand at the back of the line. Misty Mountain was rarely anything other than busy. The café was inside a renovated Quonset hut, one of many scattered throughout Alaska and leftover from the days of World War II when Alaska had been used as strategic base. The owners had turned the utilitarian half-circle of corrugated steel into a lovely space. Decorative timber beams crisscrossed the high ceiling with colorful curtains and tablecloths adding warmth to the space. Artwork adorned the walls.

Ginger pulled her mittens off and tucked them in her coat pocket. She felt a tap on her shoulder and turned to find Delia right behind her. Delia grinned. "Hey! Sorry I'm a few minutes late."

Ginger glanced at the clock above the door. "I didn't even notice," she replied with a shrug. "You're the punctual one. I'm the one who's usually skidding in somewhere late."

Delia laughed and nudged her on the shoulder. Ginger turned to see the cluster of customers in front of her had cleared out, and it was her turn to order. She perused the chalkboard menu quickly. "I'll have the house coffee and a bagel with salmon cream cheese." She turned to Delia. "I'm buying, so go ahead and order."

Delia started to shake her head, so Ginger turned to the young woman at the register. "Just make that two of everything."

"Sometimes I forget how stubborn you can be," Delia grumbled though she graciously gave in to Ginger's insistence on paying.

They stepped away from the counter to wait for their coffees. "You cook all day every day, so I figure you shouldn't be buying food somewhere else. It's a small treat, so shut up about it," Ginger said. She scanned the room and noticed a couple getting up from one of the tables by the windows. "You mind grabbing that table?" she asked, gesturing toward it. "I'll wait for our coffee and bagels."

"Got it," Delia said over her shoulder as she headed to the table. Delia being Delia, she immediately tidied the table and wiped it down with a napkin. Ginger laughed to herself when she saw one of the waitresses run over and thank

Delia when they grabbed the neat stack of dishes to cart away.

A few moments later, Ginger set their coffee and bagels on the table and slipped into the chair across from Delia. She immediately took a welcome sip of coffee and sighed. "So good. I forgot to pick up coffee beans at the grocery store over the weekend and ran out yesterday. I had to get through the entire morning at school on the shitty coffee from the break room."

"If there's one huge advantage to my job, it's that there's always amazing coffee on hand. I ordered a new espresso machine, and it's insane," Delia said, her eyes widening for emphasis as she took a bite of her bagel.

"You'll have to make me an espresso next time I'm up there, so I can test drive it for you."

Delia chuckled. They ate quietly for a few minutes. Ginger considered that she'd been more absentminded than usual the past few days, most likely because Cam was crowding her thoughts. After another few sips of coffee, her brain sharpened enough she felt like she could focus again. Delia set her cup of coffee down and leaned her elbows on the table. "So, I noticed Cam stayed somewhere else the other night," she said without preamble.

Ginger felt heat rush into her face. She bit her lip to keep from laughing. The whole thing was so ridiculous. She was deep into Cam, but so skittish about it, she wanted to hide it. "Did you now?" she countered.

Delia arched a brow and took another swallow of her coffee. "Don't be silly. I can guess where he was."

Ginger sighed and leaned back in her chair. "Fine. He was at my place last night."

Delia started to smile, and Ginger held a hand up. "Don't go getting all excited. I don't know what the hell is going on with me, or with us. This whole thing is crazy."

Delia's smile faded. "What's so crazy about it?"

Ginger looked away, staring out the window. The wind scudded across the bay, ruffling the surface of the water. A few boats were visible, and the snow-capped mountains were bright against the blue sky. Her chest felt tight with anxiety and uncertainty. This was why she'd thought it was perfectly reasonable to never have a relationship again after her divorce. She hated these feelings—the confusion, the vulnerability, the worry about how someone else felt about her. She never, ever wanted to watch her self-worth get flushed down the toilet when someone else's rejection of her made her question everything about herself. When she looked back at Delia, Delia's warm blue eyes were waiting. Her understanding was so evident, it made Ginger want to cry. She took a shaky breath and wrapped her hands around her coffee mug, the warmth anchoring her.

"It's crazy because this wasn't supposed to happen. After everything fell apart with Tony, I decided it was best to stay single. Marley said that was crazy, but it didn't seem like it to me. I can honestly say I haven't been interested in anyone at all. It was easy-peasy. Until Cam showed up in town," she said with a rueful smile.

Delia laughed softly. "Cam's hard not to notice."

Ginger threw a hand up in exasperation. "Tell me about it. It's so damn annoying that I had to go and start falling for a guy who has half the women in this town drooling over him. You should've heard Becky in the break room last week. Then, she saw him sitting beside me when we were up at the lodge the other night, and she asked all kinds of nosy questions after that."

Delia almost spit her coffee out with a laugh. She snagged her napkin and wiped her mouth. "I know all about that problem. Maybe Garrett's not your cup of tea, but it drove me crazy at first to try to deal with how damn handsome he is. He doesn't even notice it, but everywhere we go, women are eying him. It's not a jealousy thing, but it's just…

a thing. Even now, sometimes I can't believe a guy like him would want to be with me."

"Are you kidding?" Ginger asked, incredulous Delia was so oblivious to how amazing she was. "Garrett's lucky to have you. You're one of the best people I know, you're an amazing mother and friend, you're smart and independent, and on top of it all you're beautiful."

Delia shrugged. "You're one of my best friends. You're supposed to say that kind of stuff. I wasn't making the point because I needed you to shore me up, but because I wanted you to know I get it. Cam doesn't do a thing for me, but objectively speaking, he's handsome as all get out. The man is in some serious shape too."

Ginger's mind flashed back to the feel of his hard body against hers. Heat zipped through her. She took a gulp of coffee and twirled a lock of hair around her finger. "It's not just that. I don't know what to do. I didn't expect this, and I'm pretty sure he didn't either. He's only here for this season, so it's not a good idea for me to get my hopes up for anything. What's making me crazy is I wasn't having any trouble staying out of messy stuff with men and now I'm smack in the middle of it. I don't want this."

"No one likes the emotional stuff. It's messy and scary. Maybe you don't want it on an intellectual level, but clearly you do want this or it wouldn't be happening."

Ginger stared across the table at Delia and contemplated throwing something at her. Sometimes the obvious was annoying. She opted for a good strong glare, which elicited a grin from Delia.

"What? Cranky because I pointed out the obvious? Come on. If you didn't want Cam, we wouldn't be having this conversation."

Ginger sighed. "I know. I just can't help worrying if it would be best if I put a stop to it. I've never done the whole casual dating thing well. If you wondered why I married

Tony straight out of college, that was it. It seemed like we had a good thing, and I didn't want to try to keep looking. This thing with Cam is not how I do things."

"Maybe you need to stop thinking like that. There is no right or wrong way to go about it."

"Yeah, but I don't want to fall for him and have to wish I hadn't when he leaves." Her chest tightened and her stomach felt hollow.

CHAPTER 13

Cam came to a smooth stop on his skis by the trailhead. He carefully stepped to the side of the trail and glanced over his shoulder. Gage came flying down the trail and lifted a pole in a wave as he approached Cam. His speed slowed naturally as he came around the slight bend in the trail, and he stopped a few feet beyond Cam.

"Damn! The trails are great," Gage said with a wide grin.

Cam chuckled. "Thought you'd like a quick run through."

Gage walked on his skis to turn to the side and rest on one of his ski poles. "Can't believe you guys got these ready that fast."

Cam shrugged. "I'll work as hard as anyone, and Don's hard to keep up with. He wanted to make it happen, so we did. If Marley hadn't ordered the trail signs behind your back, we wouldn't be able to open them up to skiers, but she was a step ahead of you."

Another grin cracked Gage's face. "She says I'm almost impossible to surprise. The signs look great. No way anyone can get lost with all the markers."

Lost skiers on backcountry trails was a common concern at any ski lodge. Unlike downhill skiers who stuck to the well-groomed slopes, backcountry skiers went winding their way through the woods. Without marked trails, an adventurous skier could easily head off and lose track of where they were. Though the lodge had skiers sign a disclaimer to cover concerns such as that and more, no one wanted skiers to get lost in the winter on a mountain. Even in the best gear, a cold winter night could lead to hypothermia and death.

The signs from Midnight Sun Arts had a whimsical touch. The named trails were written in bright colors and artistic lettering, and the arrows guiding skiers were wild and curly. Cam nodded toward a sign nearby. "Signs can't be missed. Risa, the woman from the gallery, was hoping to hear what you thought of them. I told her you'd give her a call."

"I'll swing by the gallery tomorrow. I have to run into town to pick up a list of baby stuff." Gage shook his head slowly. "Man, I had no idea all the special stuff a baby needs."

Cam chuckled. "I bet. Haven't had one myself, but I can imagine. I wouldn't even know where to start."

"I'm flying blind, but we're doing okay. Holly makes me smile every time I look at her, so that makes it all easy," Gage offered with a wry grin. "You ready to head back down?"

"Sure. I tend to head in once the sun starts to set," Cam said with a nod toward the horizon. The days were gradually getting longer as they marched into February, but the sun still set much earlier than Cam was accustomed to. It was close to four in the afternoon, and the sun was already dipping down behind the mountains in the distance. The spruce trees looked as though they were dusted with gold from the angled rays of the sun.

Gage's eyes glanced to the sun and back again. "Just about when I get used to the short days, they start to get longer again. When I first moved back here, the short days in the winter and long days in the summer were hard to adjust to. I'm still working on it though. It's only my second year here."

"I keep forgetting that. Gotta say, you've done an amazing job with the lodge. It's hard to believe this is only your second season since you reopened."

"Couldn't have done any of it without Don and Delia. Between the two of them, they knew so much from when my grandparents ran the place that it made things a lot smoother."

"I bet. Don loves this place. He still tells me how glad he is you came back and opened it up after your grandmother passed away. I'm sure someone else has already mentioned it, but it means a lot to him to be able to work here again."

Gage nodded. "I keep trying to make sure he knows how much it means to me that he's here. Seriously, without him, it would have taken me at least another year or more to have this place open. He stepped in and made sure I didn't do anything stupid." At that, Gage turned forward on the trail and pushed off on his skis, calling over his shoulder as he did. "Beat you to the lift!"

Cam chuckled and adjusted his gloves before gripping his poles and pushing off behind Gage. Gage might not have been a competitive skier, but he was naturally fast and liked challenging others to races. They were on a fairly level stretch of the trail that connected them back to the ski lift. Cam was counting on passing Gage by jumping the stream crossing ahead. Adrenaline surged through him when he leaned into a wide curve before the view opened up from the trees into a small field. He was gaining on Gage, so he leaned forward and skied as fast as he could, savoring the burn in his legs. As he predicted, Gage aimed for the bridge that crossed the stream. The stream was on the wide side of what Cam thought he could clear, but he hadn't been a competitive skier for nothing. Even in fun, he wanted to win. He angled across the field and flew through it, tightening into a curl to push off his poles and clear the stream. He made it, but just barely, and he felt the back of his skis dip against the embankment. A familiar rush of exhilaration coursed through him as he skied away, gliding on the momentum from his jump.

He heard Gage laughing from behind when they met again where the trail narrowed into the trees. Cam lifted his ski pole in a victory wave as they slowed down before they entered the area where the lift was. Gage was only a few feet behind him when they reached the clearing and came to a stop. "I'm noticing if I want to beat you I'm gonna have to strategize."

Cam shrugged. "Maybe. You're damn fast though."

They skied to the lift and rode it down together. When they reached the bottom, Gage headed straight for the back deck when he saw Marley leaning against the railing with Holly in her arms. Cam paused and looked around. He took a deep breath of the cold air and savored the scent of snow, spruce and the hint of ocean. Skiers milled about him. For the first time in a long time, he'd raced and hadn't even thought of Eric. It was nothing more than a silly race between friends, but those kinds of races had comprised hours and hours of his childhood with his brother. Gage probably thought nothing of it, but his penchant to challenge anyone nearby to a race was incidentally helpful for Cam.

He watched as a woman who looked remarkably like Marley walked across the sprawling deck and stopped beside Marley and Gage. Gage stood beside Marley, his arm thrown over her shoulder. Cam's chest squeezed—an odd sense of longing washing through him. Last Frontier

Lodge was doing funny things to him. He'd hoped to find a place where he could enjoy skiing without being bombarded with familiar places and memories of his brother. The lodge had given him that easily. What he hadn't expected was how quickly he'd be welcomed into the friends and family that were the heartbeat of the lodge. Diamond Creek itself was also easy for him to settle into. It had all the warmth and tight-knit feeling of a small-town, but the bonus of amenities and shopping to cater to tourists.

As he watched Gage and Marley, he wondered what it would be like to have what they had. Ginger instantly flew to mind. She was almost always in his thoughts these days. Of all the things he'd hoped to find in Alaska, a woman who called to him like no other hadn't even crossed his radar. He had no idea what to do about that, in particular how much he wished he could simply enjoy what was happening with her. Moment to moment when he was with her, he could. It was when he wasn't that he stumbled and fumbled along in his thoughts. He shook his head sharply and pushed off on his skis.

Moments later, he tugged off his outer gear and hung it up in the room off the back hallway set aside for staff, family and friends to leave their gear and equipment. Walking into the kitchen, he headed straight for the hot cider Delia kept in the back corner and found Marley and the woman he'd seen on the deck beside her.

Marley smiled warmly when he approached. "Cam, this is my sister Lacey," she said nodding towards the woman beside her.

Lacey shared Marley's auburn hair and green eyes. She finished ladling cider into a mug and held her hand out. Her grip was strong and confident. "Nice to meet you. Rumor has it you're a hell of a skier," she said with a grin.

He shrugged. "It's what I do. Mind if I get some cider?"

Marley laughed. "Cam's as addicted as the rest of us to Delia's cider."

Lacey immediately set her mug down and filled another for him. "Here you go. Marley tells me you've been here for almost a month now and you've already got classes going for kids and finished the backcountry course. Not to be weird, but you're the Cam Nash who used to win all the telemark races pretty much everywhere, right?"

Cam nodded. "That would be me."

Lacey grinned. "Awesome! I'm not a professional, but I do hard-core guiding trips—I've done it in the winter for years. You and your brother are legends for those of us who pay attention to that kind of thing. I've always said back-country skiing is way harder than downhill. I've never understood why that gets all the attention."

He shrugged, a flicker of tension running through him at the passing mention of his brother. He took a breath and let the feeling wash through him. "Go figure. I'd rather not have it be any more high-profile because it makes it more fun." He took a swallow of cider and savored the warmth.

"Is your brother still competing?" Lacey asked.

Her question was natural and expected if she knew anything about them. Not many people knew about Eric's death beyond friends and family since this was the first winter since he'd died. Cam waited for the dread to roll through him, but it didn't. He was still sad, and he still missed Eric and probably would forever, but he could actually hear his name and deal with it. He met Lacey's eyes and shook his head. "Eric died in a car accident towards the end of winter last year."

Lacey's eyes widened. "I'm so sorry. I didn't know," she said softly.

"It's okay. You couldn't have known. I've had some time to get used to it." As he said the words, he realized they were finally becoming true. He'd been saying he was getting used to it for months, but it was only the last month where he could mean it. The sharp pain, almost unbearable in the early days after Eric died had softened, and the weight of guilt wasn't quite as heavy.

Lacey nodded slowly. "Well, um, okay. I'm really sorry."

"No problem. No need to dwell. Are you here for a visit?"

Lacey sighed and shook her head. "No. I live here, but like I said I do backcountry guiding for work. I decided this would be the last winter I'd do any winter trips, but leave it to me to get delayed up north because of the weather. We were out on a dog sledding trip in the Arctic Wildlife Refuge and got snowed in three days in a row. I'm so pissed because I missed Holly's birth." Lacey glanced to Marley. "I can't believe I missed it."

Marley shook her head. "Stop worrying about it. You had booked that trip before I was even pregnant. Trust me, I don't think watching me go through labor was too much fun anyway."

"Well, I feel bad, but I'm so happy to be home now. Holly looks amazing. Where did Gage take her anyway?" Lacey asked as she looked around the kitchen.

Marley gestured to the swinging door that led into the restaurant. "He's probably out there passing her around."

Lacey glanced to Cam. "Nice to meet you. I'm going to chase down my niece." At that, she turned away and walked across the kitchen into the restaurant.

Cam stepped to the cider and refilled his mug. Marley caught his eyes when he looked up. "I should've filled Lacey in about your brother. Sorry about that," she said softly.

"It's fine. It really is. I'm getting used to being asked about him, which is probably a good thing."

Marley nodded slowly. "Okay." She paused for a moment, a small smile curling her lips when she spoke again. "You'd better get ready for Lacey to want to race. She and Gage take turns racing each other all the time."

Cam leaned his head back with a mock groan. "Is there anyone Gage doesn't try to race?"

Marley grinned and shook her head before she turned to walk away. She glanced over her shoulder. "See you at dinner."

CHAPTER 14

Ginger caught the pacifier when it fell out of Holly's tiny mouth. "Got it," she said softly. Holly was sound asleep, her breath coming in small puffs. Ginger gently dropped the pacifier on the table beside the couch and looked over at Marley who was seated on the other end of the couch typing away on her laptop. "She's totally out," Ginger said.

Marley stopped typing and looked up with a smile. "She's like that. One second she's awake, the next she's dead to the world. I wish I could fall asleep like that."

Ginger stroked her index finger through the downy fuzz on the top of Holly's head. "How is she sleeping at night now?"

Marley set her laptop on the coffee table and leaned back into the corner of the couch. "So, so," she replied, flipping a hand back and forth. "Some nights are better than others, but I'm lucky if I get four straight hours. She's only a few weeks old, so I figure we're lucky if we get more than an hour at a time."

"How's Gage handling it?"

"Oh, he's great. I never thought about it before, but his days as a Navy SEAL mean he can function pretty damn well without much sleep. He said when they were on missions, they slept in fits and starts, so he learned to crash fast and wake up in a snap. He gets up as much as I do during the night. It's funny because we try to take turns if Holly wakes up, but it doesn't really matter because we're both up anyway."

Holly started to tilt heavily to one side, so Ginger carefully shifted her into the pillowed infant seat between her and Marley on the couch for this purpose. Holly didn't bat an eye, and immediately settled into her cushiony seat with a gurgle and a sigh. Marley lifted a soft fleece blanket off the back of the couch and laid it over Holly.

Ginger felt a pang in her chest. It was so sweet to watch Marley with Holly. It made her long for something she'd thought she was past wanting. When she'd married Tony right after college, she'd figured they'd have children. She hadn't gotten too specific in her hopes. They'd both attended college in Washington, and Tony had moved to Alaska with her, but he'd wanted to start in Anchorage so he could more easily find work. She should've seen the red flags at the time. He'd resisted moving to Diamond Creek, but she'd been happy to stay in Anchorage for a while because she was in the midst of applying for graduate programs. Her loosely formed hopes had splintered when Tony stopped even bothering to hide his extracurricular relationships. After she made her simple decision not to get involved with anyone ever again, she'd washed her hands of any ideas about having a family. With Cam having blown down the doors guarding her heart, she was getting emotional about all kinds of things. Including babies. As the cracks in her defenses widened, she felt more and more vulnerable. She didn't want to want something she might not be able to have.

Marley stood up and stretched. "Want something to drink? We've got water and apple juice."

Ginger glanced up, relieved for the interruption in her train of thought. "Just some water."

While Marley walked to the kitchen adjacent to the living room, Ginger looked out through the windows that ran the length of the room. Marley and Gage's private quarters were above the restaurant. They had an expansive living room with the kitchen and dining room to one side. A short hallway led to the bedrooms in the back. The windows looked out over the mountains with a clear view of the ski slopes. Kachemak Bay was visible to the side with the sun striking sparks on its surface this afternoon. Having grown up in Diamond Creek, the mountains and the bay were almost a part of Ginger. She felt soothed simply looking outside.

She scanned the slopes, wondering if she could pick Cam out of the skiers on the mountain. *Wow. How bad can this get? You're staring out the window hoping to see him skiing somewhere. Are we back in high school now?* She mentally shook herself, trying to shut up her sarcastic inner critic. She couldn't stop her eyes from scanning the slopes and smiled when she saw Cam. She knew without a doubt it was him because of his speed and grace. He easily wove through a cluster of skiers where two slopes met. Once clear, he curled forward and headed straight down the slope. The snow swirled up around him when he came to a swift stop at the base of the mountain.

Marley walked back over and set a glass of water down on the coffee table. She followed Ginger's gaze out the window and slowly grinned. "Ah, watching Cam ski is a thing of beauty."

Ginger flushed and tore her eyes away from Cam. It was ridiculous to be staring at him like this. He wasn't even near her and seeing him got her flustered. The days and nights kept rolling by, and she couldn't seem to go more than a few days without a taste of him. She was constantly teetering on the edge of asking him how he felt about her, or what he wanted. She chickened out every time. While she couldn't seem to control her attraction to him, she wasn't ready to try to discuss anything. The chemistry snapped and crackled between them, its own living and breathing force. It burned so hot and fast, all she could do was dive headfirst into it. Running away didn't seem to be an option. She knew they were approaching a point where she needed to find a way to think about what she wanted and make some sort of attempt to talk about it. For now, she kept reminding herself not to think of this as anything other than temporary.

Marley cleared her throat. Ginger snagged her water and took a gulp. "What?" she asked when Marley arched a brow.

"Aside from the fact Cam's fun to watch ski, how's it going with him?"

"What do you mean?"

Marley sighed and absently rubbed the edge of Holly's blanket between her fingers. "Seems like you two have been spending a bit of time together. I'm not asking to be nosy, but you're my best friend and I want to know how you're doing."

Ginger sighed and hooked her elbow over the armrest. "I know you're not just being nosy. Well, I mean, you *are*," she threw a grin Marley's way "but I understand why. If I knew how it was going, I'd say so. I'm all mixed up in my head. We've been spending time together…"

"Between the sheets?" Marley asked with a sly grin.

Ginger rolled her eyes. "Where else?" she countered before returning to where she left off. "Anyway, I don't know. I can't seem to think straight, but I can't stay away from him either. You had your brilliant idea that maybe I just thought he was hot like everyone else who lays eyes on him. Problem is that doesn't seem to be working. I mean, I think it's more than that. I hate this. I'm all worried what he's thinking and I'm constantly questioning myself and…"

Marley reached across Holly and rested her hand on Ginger's shoulder. "Breathe," she said softly.

Ginger, whose words had been tumbling out of her mouth, paused and took a deep breath. "Good idea," she said ruefully. "See, this is exactly why I decided it was best not to try to deal with relationships again. It makes me feel half-crazy in my head." She took another gulp of water and set it back on the coffee table.

Marley gave Ginger's shoulder a squeeze before her hand dropped to stroke Holly's head. "Okay, right. You're running in circles in your brain. How do you feel when you're with Cam?"

Therein lay the rub. When Ginger was with Cam and not caught up in ruminating about what was happening, she felt…good. He had a low-key, quiet sense of humor and was easy to be around. Whenever he spoke of his family, it was clear he loved them. Watching him here only endeared him to her more. He was amazing with the kids he taught and had somehow blended in seamlessly with the friends who made up her closest circle. Adding it all up together, and she started to get a slightly queasy feeling in her stomach.

It was bad enough she had to adjust to the reality that she wasn't immune to being attracted to someone. Cam had thoroughly disproved her of that illusion. Even worse, the sex with him was mind-bogglingly good. Good didn't even come close to capturing what sex with Cam was like if she was being honest with herself. All of that and she *liked* him, she *really* liked him. And it terrified her. She glanced to Marley and sighed. "That's the problem. I feel great when I'm with him." Then, she burst into tears.

* * *

CAM STEPPED into the back hallway at the lodge and turned to kick the wet snow off of his boots. The weather was clearing, but a snowstorm had blown through this morning and left wet, heavy snow behind. He'd spent the last few hours helping Don and Gage groom the slopes and trails and clear the wet snow off of the lifts and away from any entrances. The sun had broken through the clouds within the last hour, and the skiers had come out of the lodge in force. Cam was covered in damp snow. After he stepped into the room at the end of the hall, he kicked off his boots and left them to dry atop a rack with a drain underneath specifically to allow the melting snow to drain away instead of leaving a puddle on the floor. He peeled off his hat, gloves, and outer gear, shaking everything thoroughly. He grabbed a towel from his locker and dried off before making his way toward his suite for a shower.

As he passed through the main reception area, his eyes caught on a flash of bright red. He turned to look through the window and saw Ginger walking up the steps, her red scarf flapping in the wind. At the moment, the reception area was empty by virtue of it being mid-afternoon with most of the guests out on the slopes. He paused by the desk. The effect Ginger had on him was making him feel more out of control than he preferred. He had hoped the attraction between them would burn off, but he was well past believing that was possible. Just now, all he had to do was see her through the window and bolt of lust shot through his body.

She tugged the heavy front door open, a gust of wind coming inside with her. She didn't notice him right away, giving him a moment to watch her unwind her scarf and brush her fingers through her wind blown hair. His heart pounded hard and fast. She glanced up and her blue eyes collided with his. A slow smile spread across her face. "Hey," she said softly.

"Hey. Didn't know you were stopping by."

She held up a bag in her hand. "Marley called for an emergency diaper run. Gage was supposed to run to the store this morning, but she said he was tied up clearing snow after the storm blew through."

As Cam was about to reply, Harry came through the archway from the restaurant. He glanced up and arched a brow when he saw them. "Hey Ginger, you here on diaper delivery?"

"Yup. They'll have enough to get through the week. Is Marley upstairs?" she asked.

Harry stepped behind the desk and powered on the computerized register. "I think so. I haven't seen her since this morning."

"Well, I'll see if I can find her." Ginger tossed a smile at both of them before she walked past Harry.

Cam watched her go and wished he knew how to categorize whatever was happening with them. They weren't trying to hide the fact they were seeing each other, but they'd yet to talk about it. It was impossible to keep it off the radar in the tight-knit world of Diamond Creek and the even tighter-knit world of Last Frontier Lodge. Problem was Cam felt like he was hurtling down a ski slope at high speed when it came to Ginger. Whenever she was near, he could hardly look away. His body had a very clear idea of what he wanted—*her*. If only he knew how to handle the feelings that went along with it.

He suddenly realized he was just standing there staring at the now empty place where Ginger had vanished. He shook his head and turned at the sound of Harry's chuckle. Harry rolled his eyes the moment Cam looked over. "You are so obvious, it hurts to watch," Harry said.

"What do you mean?"

"Maybe you haven't figured it out yet, but you are seriously into Ginger, and it's way more than casual. That's what I mean," Harry said pointedly.

Cam's stomach did a slow flip. He took the few steps to the desk where Harry was typing something into the register and leaned an elbow on it. He wasn't sure what he meant to say, but he needed someone to help clear his head. "How do you know?" he finally asked.

Harry stopped typing and leaned his hips against the desk. "It's the way you look at her. I'm no expert, but if you were just after a fling, you wouldn't look half-lost when she left the room." His eyes narrowed as he considered Cam. "What do you want?"

Cam's stomach did another slow flip. The answer came quickly—he wanted Ginger and for reasons that went far beyond the attraction burning so hot and fast between them. He wasn't ready to say that aloud just yet, in part because he was uncertain of how Ginger felt. "Wish I knew what she wanted." The words slipped out.

"Well, maybe you should ask her."

Cam shook his head with a rough laugh. "Now, that's too obvious."

"Maybe, but that's what people do when they're in a relationship."

"Is that what we're in?" It was becoming painfully evident he needed to find a way to answer so many of his own questions.

Harry shrugged. "Looks like it to me. It might not be any of my business, but I'm surprised you two haven't set this place on fire the way you look at each other. In case no one else has mentioned it, Ginger doesn't really do casual. I was surprised as hell when I caught on to you two. I'm not sure what it means for her, but I'll repeat myself for good measure. Talk to her."

Someone called Harry's name from the restaurant. He

glanced over his shoulder and back to Cam. "Maybe you should take her to dinner somewhere other than here? That way, you'll actually have a chance to talk. It won't happen here, not with everyone around." At that, Harry gave a small wave and stepped away from the desk, striding quickly into the restaurant.

CHAPTER 15

Ginger fiddled with the placement of her silverware and took a sip of water. Cam had surprised her by suggesting they go out for dinner somewhere. She didn't know why it should be surprising, but it was. This *whatever* they had going had been compartmentalized to the lodge and occasional stays at her house. Actually going somewhere in Diamond Creek made it seem more real somehow. She felt restless and emotionally knotted up inside at the idea. He'd looked to her for a suggestion, so she'd mentioned Glacier Pizza because it had amazing pizza and she felt comfortable there. Once they were on their way, she'd had second thoughts because she worried who might see them. It was yet another layer of making their relationship real—something other than the surreal, hot nights they shared. Glacier Pizza was the most popular pizza place in Diamond Creek for locals, so it was unlikely they wouldn't run into someone they knew. Cam had stepped away from the booth to go to the restroom, so she took a look around.

Glacier Pizza was a basic restaurant, the kind of place

that looked lived in. It was low on frills and had amazing pizza. A massive brick oven stove sat in the center of the restaurant with an open kitchen surrounding it. A counter with stools circled the cooking area and booths lined the walls. The walls were decorated with photos from locals and tourists with one wall covered with license plates from all over the country. As she attempted to casually glance around the restaurant, she jumped when someone said her name. She looked over her shoulder to see Janie Stevens approaching their booth.

She breathed a silent sigh of relief. Janie might be curious, but she wouldn't gossip at work. Janie's brown hair swung in a ponytail as she strode to the booth. She stopped beside it and leaned her hip against the edge.

"Hey Janie, what brings you here?" Ginger asked.

Janie's hazel eyes glinted with her smile. "Pizza, what else? I'm guessing that's why you're here," she said.

Ginger felt heat spreading up her neck. Of course Janie was here for pizza. There wasn't any other reason to be here. She was relieved for the somewhat dim lighting. "Right. Pizza," she replied with a self-deprecating grin. "How's Stella been?" she asked, referring to Janie's adopted daughter. Janie was a long-time foster parent and had adopted Stella recently. Janie had been a few years ahead of Ginger in school, so she'd known her all of her life, but hadn't started to get closer to her until they ended up working together at school.

Janie grinned. "Stella's great. She's busy at music practice tonight, which is why I'm here. She comes out of practice starving, and I'm too tired to cook much tonight, so pizza it is." Janie's eyes widened slightly. "You wouldn't happen to be here for dinner with Cam Nash, would you?"

Ginger bit back her sigh. She *so* didn't want her feelings to be obvious, but it seemed she couldn't prevent it—within herself, or to others. Her back was to the restroom doors, but Janie was directly in line with them. "I would. Do me a favor and please don't mention it to the whole free world at work."

Janie's gaze softened, a touch of concern filling her eyes. "Of course I won't. I hate being gossiped about, so I'm not about to do it to anyone else. But if you think word won't travel, it already has. I heard you two were seeing each other. He's almost here, so I'll only say one more thing. There's nothing wrong with dating anyone. Enjoy it," she said with a quick wink.

Cam reached the booth and paused beside it with a polite smile on his face. He glanced between Ginger and Janie. Ginger gestured to Janie. "Cam, this is Janie Stevens. She's everyone's favorite first grade teacher." Ginger caught Janie's eyes and nodded to Cam. "And this is Cam Nash. He's helping Gage up at the lodge with getting the ski instruction program going and pretty much everything else."

Cam reached over to shake Janie's hand. She complied with a grin. "A handshake's a bit too formal for me, but we're probably not ready to hug yet."

Cam chuckled. "Nice to meet you. So you must work with Ginger?"

"I do, and she's everyone's favorite speech therapist. How do you like our ski lodge?"

"One of the best. I've been all over the world, and Gage has done a great job with Last Frontier Lodge. Aside from the hotel part, the slopes are great and you can't beat the view. I keep telling him he should be charging people just to ride the lifts."

Janie laughed. "True. Not many ski lodges are this close to the ocean. You get the mountains, oceans, glaciers and occasional wildlife."

Janie's name was called up at the counter. "Be right there," she called over her shoulder. "Gotta go. I'm due to pick Stella up in just a few minutes. Nice to meet you," she said, her eyes catching Cam's before she turned to Ginger. "See you around at work."

Janie dashed off, and Cam slipped into the booth across from Ginger. His amber eyes landed on her and her belly fluttered, heat suffusing her. It was beyond ridiculous that she could hardly be around him without her body vibrating with the force of her desire for him. Just as she was gathering herself, a waiter approached the table. She was relieved for the interruption. By the time they ordered, her pulse had slowed and she could manage to breathe normally. While they waited for their pizza, she sipped on wine and Cam nursed a beer. She managed to keep her heart rate under control while they chatted about her work and his latest escapades with the ski classes. His kids group had erupted into a snowball fight that couldn't be stopped the day before and only ended after Gage joined in.

Their pizza arrived, and Ginger started to relax. Between the wine and casual conversation, the edginess she felt whenever Cam was near started to ease. Funny thing was she didn't feel edgy when their hands were all over each other, but that was because the force of attraction was so strong, it was almost a relief to give in to it. So much of the time she'd spent with him was when they were surrounded by friends, which meant she didn't have to tolerate the anxiety she felt. She didn't like how vulnerable she felt with him. It made her restless.

His eyes became somber and he set his pizza down. "If someone asked you what we were doing, what would you say?"

She managed not to choke on the sip of wine she'd just taken. She'd just started to think it was a good thing they'd actually gone out for dinner like normal people and then he had to go and ask that. She set her glass down and tried to calm her pounding heart. She must have waited a tad too long because Cam spoke again.

"Did I freak you out?"

She shook her head quickly, and his mouth lifted at one corner. "I think I'd say..." She ran out of words and bit her lip. "I-I don't know."

His gaze stayed on her. Something flickered in their depths. His shoulders rose and fell with a breath. "It's just we keep doing what we're doing, but I don't know what that means. I'll be honest. I didn't expect anything like this, but it's, uh, more than I expected."

Her breath was shallow, and her stomach felt queasy. She didn't want to feel the way she did. She wanted to just enjoy what was happening and not think about the potential ramifications—not think about how much he was gradually knocking down the barriers she'd erected around her heart, not think about how every time she thought about him leaving after this winter, her heart felt almost bruised, not think about how she couldn't help but hope maybe, just maybe she could have a chance at the one thing she'd thought she'd never have...love. As long as they were drifting along, thrown together by the convenient circumstance of his job at the lodge and acting on the wild drumbeat of desire that pounded between them, it seemed like she could handle it. It was this almost surreal experience.

To have him try to put words to it made it seem real, and she wasn't so sure she could handle real. Yet, he wasn't dodging and she sensed this wasn't easy for him. She managed a somewhat full breath. "I didn't expect this either. In case you were wondering, before I met you I pretty much decided I wasn't going to do relationships. At all. Casual or not. But this...*this*...with us is hard to ignore." Her heart sped when she realized her words were tumbling out, and she was being more open than she'd meant to. He didn't need to know her past and why she decided against relationships. "If someone asked you what we were doing, what would you say?" she asked, blurting out the same question he'd asked her.

He shifted his shoulders and took a swallow of beer. "Well, Harry told me today it looked like we were in a relationship."

A laugh bubbled out. Of course Harry had to go and say something. Harry was the quiet observer of all goings on at the lodge. He didn't gossip much, but he noticed everything. "What brought that up with him?"

The slightest flush rose on Cam's angled cheekbones. "Apparently, he noticed the way I look at you. Oh, and he thinks we're going to set the place on fire," he said with a rueful smile. "I think he was trying to be helpful."

Ginger couldn't help but laugh. A sense of relief stole over her to hear Harry had noticed how Cam looked at her. She hoped maybe he was in over his head as well. "Well, was he helpful?" she asked.

"He's the one who said I should talk to you." Cam paused and took a bite of his pizza. After a moment, he spoke again. "Look, I have no idea what I'm doing here. Every time I think about not being with you, I don't like that idea at all. So, I figured maybe I should say something. If you're wondering, I've never had much of a chance for any kind of relationship. All through high school and college, I skied every spare minute I had. I started racing early and never stopped until Eric died. I didn't have any plans when I came up here other than to find somewhere to ski and maybe get my head back on straight. I met you and…well…"

Ginger was oddly relieved he ran out of words. She'd gotten over the whole speechless thing with him, but she didn't want to feel alone, the only one who was stumbling around in the dark with her feelings. His honesty warmed her, and dammit, it made her like him even more. She took a steadying breath and met those amber eyes of his that made her want to dive in. "I have no idea what I'm doing either. I'm not sure what you've heard, but I got married straight out of college. It didn't go so well. I imagine someone's said something to you about it because Diamond Creek's not exactly big, and I have friends who stick their nose in my business. I know this because I stick mine in theirs when I care. Anyway, my divorce was final just over two years ago. It's so embarrassing to be divorced before you're even thirty. So maybe I wasn't flying all over the world skiing, but I don't have much experience doing the relationship thing the right way. I've got the 'messed up, wished I'd had more sense sooner thing' down."

Her laugh held only a faint tinge of bitterness and almost no feeling left behind it. It was more habit than anything. She had learned the hard way to be careful. After she finished speaking, she anticipated that familiar feeling of vulnerability, of discomfort, but it didn't come. Instead, she was relieved. Maybe actually talking wasn't such a bad idea. She might have to thank Harry.

Cam's eyes stayed on her, somber and searching. "So we're both stumbling along then? I suppose that's a good thing," he said with a soft chuckle before his gaze sobered. "I'm sorry things didn't go well with your marriage. That must've…"

"Been a shit show," she interjected helpfully.

He angled his head to the side with a smile curling slowly across his face. "If that's your description, there you go."

She shrugged. "Sarcasm takes the edge off sometimes. Seriously, it was for the best in the end, but it doesn't change the reality that I'm not any more experienced at this than you. I guess neither of us expected this, and here we are."

He nodded slowly and took another bite of pizza. She took a gulp of wine and leaned back, the tension slowly easing from her shoulders. She thought perhaps they'd talked enough for tonight. She was so relieved she wasn't turning into a ball of stress over it, she wanted to quit while she was ahead. "I think we've talked enough for now."

His eyes widened and a slow smile followed. "Alright then."

Feeling playful and emboldened, she kicked his shin under the table. He kicked right back, and she burst out laughing. Over the next few minutes, she sipped her wine while conversation moved onto lighter territory. The waiter came to clear their plates and topped off her wine. While she was chatting with the waiter about Diamond Creek's local baseball league, she felt Cam's palm slide up her thigh and had to force herself to hold still. He dragged his fingers slowly along the inside of her thigh, his touch hot through her leggings. Her face heated, liquid need spinning inside of her and moisture drenching her panties.

The friendly waiter—she thought his name was Bradley —continued talking excitedly about how he hoped to make it onto Diamond Creek Batters, her old team. He appeared completely oblivious to the fact Cam was driving her nearly wild under the table. Bradley was still talking when his name was called from the bar in the center. He stopped midsentence. "Oops. I've got some pizzas to serve. You two need anything else?"

"Just the check. Take your time," Cam said with a smile. Bradley may not have noticed the wicked gleam in his eyes, but Ginger did.

When Bradley turned away, she caught Cam's eyes and shook her head. 'Stop it!" she hissed.

He shook his head. "Not yet."

His fingers, which had been teasing along her thighs, dipped between them. He stroked a finger firmly across her, the sensation sharp and sweet. Her channel throbbed, and she couldn't help but arch her hips into his touch as he dragged his fingers back and forth. When she had to bite back a moan and realized her knees had fallen apart and she was all but straining to get closer to him, she straightened in her seat and shot him a warning glance. "Behave."

Though he'd been the one driving her mad, that subtle flush had returned to his cheeks and he took a gulp of air as his hand slowly moved away. She felt the loss of his touch all the way through her. Here they were, in the middle of a restaurant, a most decidedly public place, and all she wanted was to crawl across the table and straddle him.

Her pulse carried on in its usual uncontrolled state with Cam while she tried to get her breathing under control. Cam ran a hand through his hair and leaned back. Not a word passed between them and she felt more connected to him in that moment than she ever had to anyone. Somehow their conversation earlier had made the connection between them real. The living breathing force she couldn't ignore and couldn't turn away from now had words and feelings attached to it. They weren't her words and feelings alone, so it wasn't as terrifying as she'd imagined it could be.

Bradley swept by with a pizza in one hand and their check in another. He set it on the table with a grin. "Thank you! Sure you don't need anything else?"

Cam arched a brow in question to her. She glanced up at Bradley. "We're good to go. The pizza was delicious."

"Definitely! Thank you," Cam said as he slipped the check to his side of the table and quickly looked down. In a flash, he passed over the bill with cash. "Keep the change."

"Thanks! You two come again soon," Bradley said before he swirled off.

Cam's eyes swiveled to her. "Let's go."

She looked over and almost melted into a puddle at the dark desire swirling in his gaze.

CHAPTER 16

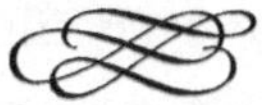

Snow started to fall on the drive to Ginger's house. Plump snowflakes floated down, illuminated in the beam of headlights. Cam turned into Ginger's driveway and came to a stop. When he turned the engine off, quiet settled around them. Since they'd left the restaurant, he'd barely been able to keep the lust pounding through his body in check. He couldn't have said what he expected from attempting to talk to Ginger, but the effect had been one of immense relief followed by a straight shot of desire. He'd looked across the table at her with her translucent blue eyes, which darkened and brightened depending on her mood, her tousled brown hair and her plump lips, and all he'd wanted to do was yank her across the table into his lap. He'd settled for teasing her under the table, only to realize his own limits. By the time they left, he'd barely gotten his hard-on under control.

The porch light was on, and it cast a soft circle of silvery light with the snow drifting down. He glanced to her, colliding with her gaze. The lust surging through him tightened its grip. "Are you coming in?" she asked, her words raspy.

"Definitely."

Her eyes darkened, and she unbuckled her seatbelt. Without a word, she opened the door to his truck and climbed out. He followed quickly. Once they were inside, she hung up her coat and kicked her boots off, gesturing for him to do the same. George bounded over to greet them. Cam had come to learn George expected a few minutes of petting. Ginger lifted him in her arms and stroked his head while she walked through the archway into the kitchen. She busied herself getting his food ready and handed George over to Cam. He sat down at the kitchen table and idly stroked George who leapt down once Ginger filled his water bowl with fresh water.

She stood and turned to Cam. "Do you want anything to drink?"

He shook his head and stood, taking two quick strides to stand just in front of her. Without preamble, he dipped his head and caught her lips in a fierce kiss. A bolt of heat shot through him as her tongue met his in a wild tangle. He tugged her close, sliding a palm down her back to cup her bottom and pull her against him. She moaned into his mouth and arched into his hips. His cock was so hard, it bordered on painful. He broke away from their kiss, his breath heaving. "Upstairs," he choked out. He latched a hand around one of hers and started to walk to the stairs.

At the base of the spiral staircase, she stepped in front of him onto the bottom stair. In slow motion, she traced his jawline and stroked a hand into his hair. The air around them was charged, beating with the pulse of desire between them. When she whispered his name, heat blazed through him. Her lips dropped to his neck where she trailed hot, wet kisses while she slipped her palms under his shirt and dragged it up. She only leaned away long enough to yank his shirt over his head and fling it across the room. Her mouth and hands traveled in a meandering path until she swiftly unbuttoned his jeans and curled her hand over his cock. He was throbbing with need, so desperate to be inside of her he could barely hang on.

"Ginger, let me..."

He felt her shake her head. *"Uh, uh. My turn."*

When he managed to drag his eyes open and look down, her gaze met his—a gleam in her eyes. She shoved his jeans around his hips and freed his cock from his briefs. She settled her hips on the step behind her and took him in her mouth. His knees buckled, and he had to grab onto the railing to hold himself up. She proceeded to drive him to the point of madness with her hot, wet mouth. She dragged her tongue along the underside of his shaft and cupped his balls lightly in one hand. She curled her other around his cock and alternated between bringing him fully into her mouth and stroking him in her wet grip.

He was on the verge of exploding when she slowly drew back and stood. Driven solely by frantic need, he hooked his hand under the hem of her shirt, lifted it swiftly and tossed it aside. He needed to see her, needed to feel her skin against his. With a flick of his thumb, her bra came undone and her breasts tumbled free. Her nipples were a deep, dusky pink and taut. He cupped a palm around one of her breasts and captured the nipple between his thumb and forefinger. Her head fell back on a small cry. He couldn't resist and leaned forward to swirl his tongue around her nipple while he shoved her leggings down around her hips, dragging her underwear along with them. She kicked her leggings free, and they twirled around the stair railing. Everything became a blur as he sucked her nipple into his mouth and plunged his fingers into the slick heat of her channel.

On the verge of madness, he tore his mouth away and

roughly turned her, stroking a hand over the soft give of her bottom and dragging his fingers into her folds. His brain was fuzzed with desire when he heard her say his name over her shoulder. "Huh?"

"I'm on the pill," she said.

He shook his head, trying to clear the haze in his brain. "Are you sure? I can..."

She rolled her eyes over her shoulder. He could see the corner of her mouth lift in a smile. "I wouldn't have said anything if I wasn't sure."

That was all he needed. He dragged his fingers once more through the pulsing, wet heat of her before gripping his cock in his hand and positioning it at her entrance. He stroked a hand down her spine, bringing his palm to rest in the sweet dip at her waist before surging into her clenching heat. With her hips rolling to meet his, he set a rhythm—slow and deep. He gripped her hip in one hand, the soft give of her skin under his fingers almost intoxicating. Need tightened inside him with each stroke and he drove deeper and faster, pounding against her. He slipped a hand around her waist, sliding over the curve of her belly and delving into her folds to stroke her clit. She arched and flexed against him, pushing her hips back into him. Her breath broke on a sharp cry. With her channel pulsing around him, he finally let go, the pressure spinning loose inside. His release crashed over him hard and fast.

He held her against him for a long moment. Their breath heaved and slowed in unison. When her body softened, he eased his hold and stepped back, immediately missing the feel of being inside of her. He dropped a kiss on the back of her neck before lifting her in his arms.

* * *

CAM GATHERED her against him and looked down. Again

and again, Ginger almost lost herself in his amber gaze—it was like honey washing over her. He started to take a step and almost lost his balance. She giggled. "Are you really going to try to carry me up a spiral staircase?"

"Of course. I've got you," he said with a low chuckle.

His hold never wavered, although their progress up the stairs was slow. He carried her straight to the bed, lifting the soft down quilt and letting it drift down over them. The rush of cool air pebbled her skin, but he immediately curled around her, the warmth of his body dispelling the momentary chill. She'd left the curtains open this morning, and the stars spread out across the sky in their glittering glory.

"Wow, it's beautiful out," Cam said.

His voice was a low rumble against her neck.

"It is. I like to leave the curtains open just for that." The moon was visible in the corner, an almost perfect curved sliver sitting pretty above the mountains. Even in darkness, the hulking shapes of the mountains could be seen. The surface of the bay shimmered under the soft light cast by the moon.

Ginger rested in Cam's arms and felt her heart slowly settle. His palm was resting on the curve of her hip, the warmth anchoring her. After losing herself in him and in the wild storm between them, she savored the feel of him beside her. An aching sweetness stole through her when his lips landed softly on her neck.

CHAPTER 17

Cam felt the vibration of his phone in his pocket. He'd stopped to check on a skier who'd seriously overestimated his skills and tried to jump the stream. Of course, the young man had landed shy of the other side and tumbled onto the ice. The skier was fine, but bruised and with a broken ski. After getting the radio call, Cam had ridden up with Don on the snowmobile. He sent the skier back down and was in the middle of a quick loop on the trails when his phone buzzed. He skied to a stop by the start of the trails and slipped his phone out to see Ivy's name flashing on the screen.

"Hey Ivy, what's up?"

"Hey Cam! Guess what?"

Cam smiled wryly, but he went along with Ivy's question. "What?"

"I'm at the airport in Homer, and I need a ride."

"Huh? What are you doing in Alaska?"

"Well, I wanted to surprise you, but I didn't realize Homer was over a hour away from Diamond Creek. The cab ride is pricey, although I can't even believe there's a cab to drive me that far in Alaska," she said with a small laugh "so I'm calling you. I know you're busy, but I can wait until you can get here."

Cam couldn't help but laugh. Leave it to his big-hearted sister to try to surprise him and miscalculate. Ivy was probably the smartest person he knew, but she didn't pay attention to details outside of her academic research. "Of course, I'll come get you. All I need is time to get off the mountain and drive down there. I can probably be there within two hours. Will that work?"

"Of course. I've got my laptop. I'll sit tight here and do some work while I wait. Take your time."

Cam skied straight for the quickest route downhill, flew down it and came to a swirling stop at the foot of the mountain. He headed inside and ran into Gage while he was putting his gear away.

Gage stepped into the back room and leaned against the wall. "Don said the kid's fine. If all we have is one broken ski this month and a few bruises, I'll take it. He's a little embarrassed. I told him even I haven't been able to clear that stream yet," he said with a grin.

Cam chuckled. Ski resorts dealt with injuries with some frequency. It was usually minor, but a few broken bones here and there weren't unusual. Visitors signed waivers because skiing came with inherent risks. Gage went the extra mile and had established a good relationship with the hospital, along with a local doctor's office that provided non-emergency care for a contract fee.

"It's been a good season so far. I'll take it too. Hey, my sister just called. She decided to try to surprise me with a visit, but she didn't realize the Homer airport was over an hour away. Everything's done for today, so I thought I'd go pick her up. Anything you need me to do before I take off?"

"Of course not. Get going as soon as you can. You think she'll want to join us for dinner in the lodge?"

"Oh yeah. Ivy was planning to come up anyway, but she's just here a little early. She'll want to know everyone and everything. She's my little sister, but she thinks she's my big sister."

Gage grinned and pushed away from the wall. "Great. I'll see you later then."

Cam followed him down the hall and raced upstairs for a quick shower and a change of clothes. Once he was in his truck, he put his phone on speaker and called Ginger. She was at work, so he knew she wouldn't answer, but he wanted her to know Ivy was here. She startled him by answering.

"Hey," she said brightly.

"Hey. Didn't expect you to pick up."

"The student I usually see this period is out sick today, so it's just me. I saw it was you, so…"

He could feel the smile in her words, and he smiled in return. All he had to do was hear Ginger's voice and it made his day.

"So what's up? You don't usually call when I'm at work."

"Oh, right. I wanted to let you know my sister Ivy decided to come for a surprise visit. I'm headed to Homer to pick her up at the airport now."

"That's great! I know you were hoping she'd come visit this winter. Do you think she'll be up for dinner at the lodge tonight?"

"Definitely. I was hoping you'd come by."

What went unsaid was the fact that they'd been seeing each other almost every night since their pizza date. He didn't want to make assumptions about how she might feel about meeting his family though.

"Of course! I'll head up after I swing by the house to check on George."

"Perfect. I'll see you then."

He heard a loud bell in the background over the line.

"Time to go. My next student will be here any minute. See you later," Ginger said before hanging up.

When the line clicked silent, Cam took a breath and let it out. For a split second, he'd wanted to tell her he loved her. The words almost slipped out. He hadn't even thought about it. His heart pounded wildly in a delayed reaction. He'd fallen so hard and fast, he hadn't even seen it coming. He gulped in air and tried to get a hold of himself. Ginger had come to mean so much to him. As the recognition of what he'd been about to say sunk in, he realized it felt exactly right. He didn't want to scare her, but he desperately wanted to know how she felt. Much as he'd like to think he'd find a way to talk to her soon, with Ivy here, he didn't know if he would. Maybe that was a good thing. He needed time to think about when and how to tell Ginger how he felt.

The drive went by in a blur and before he knew it, he was cresting the hill into Homer. The town spread out before him. It was late afternoon with the sun dipping down in the sky. Homer was nestled against the hills toward the end of the Kenai Peninsula. One could see to the head of Kachemak Bay here with the mountains curving around the bay. Cam hadn't been to Homer yet, although many locals in Diamond Creek kept suggesting he visit. Diamond Creek's airport was tiny and couldn't accommodate the larger commercial flights, so many travelers flew to Homer and drove north from there. He followed signs to the airport and parked.

When he walked in, the airport was quiet from the lull between flights. He glanced around and saw Ivy over in a corner. She was typing away on her laptop, oblivious to everything around her. He strode over and stopped in front of her.

"Ivy," he said.

Her eyes flew up. "Cam!" She shoved her laptop into the seat beside her and scrambled up.

He caught her in his arms, hugging her tightly. When she stepped back, her clear amber gaze was warm and searching. Ivy was the heart and soul of their family. She always had been. After Eric died, she'd tried to wrap everyone in her arms. Cam had needed her then and still did, but he had his feet back under him and the sharp pain of his grief had dulled. He would always miss Eric and imagined he would continue to heal, but he'd found the ability to experience joy again. He met Ivy's gaze and arched a brow. "I'm doing okay. You can stop worrying."

Ivy sighed and threw her hands up. "I get to worry all I want. Let's go."

* * *

GINGER SAT at her kitchen table with George on her lap. She'd gotten home after school and ended up cleaning her entire house. It wasn't that her house was all that big, but she generally took a slapdash approach to housecleaning. The house practically sparkled now. *Maybe you should get this nervous more often. It's damn good for getting things done.* A soft laugh slipped out. Her internal snide remarks were on point. She was only just starting to get used to the fact she and Cam were more than a passing fling. She'd been so internally resolved to never be in a relationship again, it had taken some mental gymnastics to keep from constantly freaking out inside. Now, his sister was here for a visit. Meeting family made things feel…real. Her thoughts were running rampant. She couldn't' help but wonder what he might have said to his sister about them and about her. She was tied up in knots over whether she should try to play it casual and act like they were just friends. *Oh my God. Stop it.*

*Just stop the madness. You're a grown up. All you need to do is be yourself and act normal. *mental pause* What's normal?*

She'd thought she was doing the 'normal' thing when she married Tony and look how well that went. *Cam is nothing like Tony and you know it.* That was her heart talking, which still had to practically shout to be heard over her well-honed defenses. She knew her heart was right on that point though. Trust was a bit of a hang up for her. Yet, even though she was tied up inside over Cam, she trusted him. While she wasn't yet certain about his feelings for her, she trusted he would be honest with her. That's just how he was. She wanted that trust to comfort her, but it almost made it harder—because it made him that much more appealing.

She sighed and lifted George's ears in her hands, gently rubbing the insides, which he loved. His wide blue eyes stared at her for a moment before he wrinkled his nose and shook his head when she let his ears fall. Over twenty minutes ago, she'd run out of things to clean in the house and given George fresh water and his evening food. She'd yet to marshal the courage to stand up from the kitchen table and leave her house to drive to the lodge—a simple trip that she took so often she could probably drive there blindfolded and not miss a turn. She took a deep breath and tried to ease the anxiety knotted in her chest. George leapt down from her lap and bounded into the living room. She forced herself to stand and leave.

A short while later, she pulled into a parking spot at the ski lodge. After she turned the engine off, silence settled around her. She looked out over the bay, her eyes scanning across the mountain peaks on the far side and out over the water. It was early evening and Mount Augustine stood tall and majestic in the waters. It was the lone volcano visible from this vantage point. At the moment, it peak was arrayed with clouds shot through with orange and gold from the setting sun. After a few moments, she gathered the threads of her courage and climbed out of her car.

When she entered the lodge, Marley was standing by the reception desk with Holly in her arms and talking with Harry. She turned to the door and smiled. "Hey Ginger! I was hoping you'd make it tonight. Cam's sister is here. Have you met her yet?"

Harry gave Ginger a wave and called out. "I'm headed back to the kitchen. See you ladies in a bit."

Ginger walked to Marley's side and dropped a quick kiss on Holly's forehead. Before she said a word, Marley's eyes narrowed with concern. She hadn't been Ginger's best friend for most of their lives for nothing. "What's wrong? You look, I don't know, off or something."

Ginger bit her lip. "What does 'off' mean?"

Marley adjusted Holly in her arms. ""I don't know. Tense?"

"Oh, I'm definitely tense. Cam asked me if I'd be up tonight because Ivy's here. Of course I said I would and I want to meet her, but I'm completely freaking out now." Since they were alone, her words tumbled out. If anyone could help her make sense of her personal freak out, it would be Marley.

Marley lifted an arm and tugged Ginger into a quick hug from the side. "Okay, no big deal. I'm guessing meeting Cam's sister might be weird. Is that it?"

Ginger chewed her lip and shrugged. "It makes things seem really real. I know we haven't had tons of time to talk since you had Holly, but things have kind of..." she paused and gestured her hand in a circle "...moved along with Cam and I. I had my own little freak out about that, but Delia talked me down. And then last week, Cam and I actually talked..." She paused and blushed furiously when Marley arched a brow and grinned. "You can tease all you want, but you had to figure your own stuff out with Gage, so cut me some slack. Plus, you and Gage are perfect together and it worked out just like it was supposed to. I don't even know what's going to happen with me and Cam and now I'm meeting his sister and who knows what she's going to think and I don't..."

Marley held a hand up, and Ginger gulped in a breath of air. Her stomach was tied in knots and she was talking so fast, she'd forgotten to breathe.

"Okay, so this is a big deal. That's okay. I was pretty nervous when I met Gage's family," Marley said.

"Yeah, but you two are together, together."

Marley angled her head to the side, her eyes narrowing. "So are you and Cam. Maybe we haven't had a ton of time to talk, but I'm not blind. It's super obvious Cam is way, way into you."

"Really?" Ginger couldn't help but ask and then blushed even harder at what her question revealed—her deep insecurity about whether a man like him could be into her, and just how into him she was. If only she didn't care, but she cared—way, way, way too much. It made her feel so exposed, she could hardly tolerate the feeling.

Marley's eyes softened. "Yes, really. Do I have to remind you again that you're totally a catch? You're smart, gorgeous and one of the best people I know. Cam isn't stupid. He totally gets you."

Ginger took a deep breath and shook her head. "I need an off-switch for my brain. If I could just stop worrying and thinking, I wouldn't be so crazed."

Marley laughed softly. "If only we all had one of those. I can still talk myself in circles on a bad day. Gage and I are solid, but it's not like doubt doesn't creep in. When I felt like a walking beached whale at the end of my pregnancy, I happened to come into the restaurant when this woman was blatantly sizing Gage up and flirting like crazy. For the next hour, I beat myself up for how crappy I looked and convinced myself Gage was only putting up with me because he thought he had to."

"Are you serious?" Ginger asked.

"What? You know how much I can worry. If there was a contest, I'm pretty sure I'd beat you," Marley said with a wry laugh.

Ginger shook her head with a laugh. "I suppose so, but Gage is totally in love with you. He probably didn't even notice that woman was flirting with him."

"Yeah, that's what he said. I'm only telling you because maybe you won't feel so silly if you know you're not the only one. Cam is totally into you. Take my word for it. Come on. Let's get in there. Even if you're nervous, you'll like Ivy."

Ginger walked beside Marley into the restaurant where they immediately veered to their usual booth in the far corner. Cam's sister couldn't be missed. She shared his amber eyes and hair. As soon as they reached the table, Ivy stood and threw her arms around Ginger. Ginger reflexively hugged her back. When Ivy stepped away, she clasped her hands together, a wide smile on her face. "It's so great to meet you! Cam told me all about you. Anyone that Cam loves that much is automatically my friend."

Ginger blushed so hard, she thought she might go up in flames. Cam was nowhere in sight. Fortunately, only Marley, Delia and Garrett were present. If she had to have a crowd for her mortification, at least it didn't include too many people.

Delia caught her eye. "Hey Ginger, have a seat," she said patting the spot beside her. Delia sat across from Garrett who had the grace to offer nothing more than a friendly smile and a wink. Ginger sat down quickly. Delia immediately held up a bottle of wine. "Wine?"

"Yes, please."

While Delia filled her wineglass, Marley asked if Ivy

needed anything else for her room.

"Nope. I'm all set. It's a beautiful room with the most amazing view ever! You didn't have to give me my own entire suite," Ivy said.

Marley shook her head. "Family comes first around here. Gage always keeps one suite vacant just in case. He's got a big family, so every once in a while we get surprise visitors." At that, she pointed to Garrett. "He's the one who started that policy when he showed up unannounced and we didn't have anywhere for him to sleep for a few nights."

Garrett shrugged. "It was worth it. I got to crash in Delia's office," he said with a sly grin.

Delia rolled her eyes. "Anyway," she said with a pointed glance at Garrett, "Marley means it. Family comes first, so don't worry about being in that suite. If you weren't here, it would be empty."

"Well, thank you." Ivy paused and looked around. "When did Cam say he would be back down here?"

Gage approached the table at that moment. "He just finished helping me unload some supplies for the kitchen. He's snagging some cider right now and should be out any minute."

Gage dropped a kiss on Marley's cheek. "Need anything from upstairs? I'm gonna run up and change."

"I'll go with you. Holly needs a diaper change, and I forgot to bring the diaper bag down."

After they departed, conversation carried on around Ginger. She was still getting to know Garrett since he'd married Delia and was coming to appreciate that he was the master at sizing up a situation and making any social setting feel comfortable. He promptly began asking Ivy what she did and offering a veritable history on Diamond Creek and the geography of southcentral Alaska.

After learning Ivy was practically a genius and was getting her graduate degree in mechanical engineering,

Ginger was more than a little relieved at Ivy's enthusiastic welcome. It wasn't that Ivy bragged about herself, but Ginger knew perfectly well that a graduate degree in mechanical engineering at UC Berkeley required near perfect grades and test scores in math and sciences. Ivy had a freshness and enthusiasm about her research that was rare. She clearly loved what she was doing. She was also fascinated with Alaskan geography, which led Garrett down the path of the local area. By the time he finished his mini spiel on where Alaska was situated in the Ring of Fire, the basin within the Pacific Ocean where over seventy five percent of the world's volcanoes were, Ginger was impressed.

"Wow, Garrett. I had no idea you knew all that. I grew up here and I didn't even know half of this stuff," Ginger said.

Delia shook her head with a laugh. "He studies everything. He asked me one morning how many volcanoes were nearby, and I knew I'd come home that night and he'd have looked it up."

Garrett grinned. "When I have questions, I like to know the answers."

The swinging door by the kitchen opened and Cam walked through. Ginger's pulse took off at a gallop. She was starting to wonder if the effect he had on her would ever lessen.

* * *

CAM WALKED down the hallway at the lodge later that night. He wasn't thrilled with the fact he wasn't going over to Ginger's place, but he didn't feel right taking off the same night Ivy arrived. Ivy had headed to her room a few minutes ago after their small dinner gathering broke up. He'd pondered asking Ginger to stay here, but before he had a chance to ask, she'd commented she needed to go home to check on George. He'd never had a pet rabbit, so he didn't quite know if George really needed that much attention. He wondered if she was simply looking for an excuse not to spend the night with him. The thought unsettled him. It was enough to accept he'd fallen in love with her and even harder to be uncertain of her feelings for him. He let himself in his suite, tossed his key card on the coffee table and plunked down on the couch. He didn't bother to turn the lights on because he liked looking out into the night sky.

The moon was high above the mountains and close to half-full. The stars were so bright here, he felt as if he could reach up and touch them. The ski slopes glimmered like silver under the moonlight. He leaned his head back against the couch and sighed. Dinner had been good. It was always good, but he was glad to have Ivy here. He thought back over all the years he'd spent traveling around with Eric and realized he and Eric had never had the same type of close relationship he shared with Ivy. Eric was so focused on racing and competing he didn't even bump up against emotional topics. Once Ivy grew up and started college, she and Cam had gradually become each other's main support within the family.

He hadn't intended to, but on the ride back to Diamond Creek from Homer, he'd ended up telling Ivy all about Ginger and how he felt. He hadn't used the word 'love' because he was still uncomfortable even thinking it himself, but he'd been open about his uncertainty. Ivy, of course, had been thrilled. Ivy was rather romantic even though she left little room for romance in her life. She was all but convinced Cam should declare his love for Ginger and ski off into the sunset with her. That thought elicited a twinge of worry. If only it was that simple. Ginger had seemed tense tonight. If it hadn't been for Ivy, he would have wanted to ask her what was wrong.

Impulsively, he tugged his phone out of his pocket and texted her.

How's George?

He stared out at the sky while he waited for her reply. An owl hooted softly in the trees by the lodge.

George is great. He's napping by the woodstove.

Ah, smart rabbit. By the woodstove is the best place to be. Ivy enjoyed meeting you.

Ivy's awesome! She looks so much like you.

So I'm told. Just wondering...everything okay with you tonight?

He didn't know how to meander his way into asking her, so he just went for it. He couldn't say why he was nervous to ask if she was okay, but he was. The pause between his text and her reply stretched out long enough that he began to worry he shouldn't have asked the question.

Think so. Kinda got anxious about meeting your sister. You know...the family thing.

Right. The family thing. Well...hope it was okay.

Of course! smh...me worrying about nothing. I'll be up for some skiing tomorrow.

This was what he hated about texting. He wanted to see her face, so he could read her expression. Was she worrying about nothing? Or was more going on? Her quick change of topic could either mean she was dismissing the topic because it was minor, or because she really didn't want to discuss it further. Without anything other than words on a phone screen, he didn't have any other cues to help him decipher.

K. Wish you were here.

G'night.

Sleep tight.

After pointlessly waiting to see if she'd say anything else for several minutes, he tossed his phone on the coffee table and went to bed.

CHAPTER 18

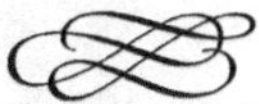

Ginger finished her last email of the day at work and hit send before closing her laptop and standing up to stretch. Mondays were usually her busiest days and today was no exception. She snagged her water bottle off the table and took several swallows before grabbing her coat and purse and heading out. She'd had a busy weekend. With Ivy visiting, Ginger had gone skiing both Saturday and Sunday. Between skiing and the casual gatherings of friends and family at the lodge, Ginger had barely had a minute to herself. The good thing about that was she hadn't had much time to obsess over Cam and just what the hell she was doing. For a little while after they'd talked, she'd managed to mentally relax—a tiny bit. Between the passage of time and her discomfort with how comfortable she was getting with Cam, she was out of sorts.

Every time she had a minute, her stomach churned and anxiety coiled in her chest. Cam was starting to mean too much to her. She was remembering how painful and disorienting it had been when her marriage fell apart. While she wasn't married to Cam, he already meant more to her than

Tony ever had. She'd thought she loved Tony, but hindsight showed her mostly she'd thought it was time to settle down. What she felt with Cam rose to another level entirely and scared the living hell out of her. Because she didn't know if her heart could take it if somehow things fell apart with them.

Snow was falling softly when she pushed through the main school doors outside. She hit her remote start and walked quickly to her car. When she got home, she saw Cam had texted her about coming over tonight. She'd side-stepped him all weekend, three entire nights, and made excuses about why she couldn't stay at the lodge. Ivy's surprise weekend visit had given her a little breathing room. Ivy had flown out this morning. A part of her was near frantic to dive into the incandescent flames between her and Cam, to nearly singe herself in his arms until she found release, and to fall asleep twined in his embrace. And that's what terrified her. She wanted him so, so, so much. It went beyond physical. Oh, she wouldn't deny sex with him was so intense, it was otherworldly. Yet, it was the emotion under-neath that fanned the flames between them.

She ignored his text for now and immediately went to the woodstove to get a fire started. The snow had started to pick up and an icy wind was coming off the bay. She wanted a warm fire and a quiet night. *And Cam. You want Cam. Precisely why I need to take some space. I can't let myself fall apart again. But Cam won't hurt you, you know that.* She shook her head sharply. Cam wasn't Tony. She didn't think he would be callous or purposefully hurtful. Yet, she had no idea if he planned to stay in Diamond Creek beyond this winter. She didn't want to pressure him, and there was no way she could consider leaving Diamond Creek. Diamond Creek was home, heart and soul to her.

She finishing setting some logs in the woodstove and tucked a few soft, frayed scraps of spruce underneath as tinder. With a flick of the lighter, the tinder caught the flame. She adjusted the damper and closed the door before standing. The snow blew against the windows. The light was fading, the gloaming of dusk taking over. The slate gray sky was nearly indistinguishable from the gray water below. She heard George hopping down the stairs and turned to follow him in the kitchen.

Hours later, she sat on the couch with her favorite fleece blanket draped over her and George napping nearby. The fire flickered through the glass door of the woodstove while the wind kept blowing off the bay, a steady drone of sound. She was watching reruns of various comedy shows and had successfully dodged Cam's request to come over by telling him she wasn't feeling good. It wasn't exactly a lie, but it wasn't for the reasons he might have assumed. He'd come to mean far too much to her, and she needed to find a way to protect her heart. She went to bed and tossed and turned through the night. Every moment she was awake, she longed for Cam.

The following morning, Ginger stood under the steaming hot water and made a decision. She would tell Cam she needed some time to herself. She didn't even know if that made sense because they hadn't defined what they were. It didn't matter because she needed to get a hold on her emotions, to corral them to a place where she could manage them.

After getting dressed and having a quick breakfast, she raced outside to get the snow off of her car and head to work. Snow in Alaska rarely meant anything closed. Unless a storm was severe, and severe in Alaska meant more than three feet of snow, everything carried on. As such, even though a foot of snow had fallen last night, school was open and buses were running on schedule. She started her car and began brushing the snow off with an industrial sized snowbrush.

She was in the middle of clearing the snow from around her tires when she heard another vehicle pull up. Expecting to see the plow guy, she glanced up to find Cam climbing out of his truck. Her heart flew into her throat. For a flash, she recalled when she first saw him. Just now, with his amber hair and eyes and his strong, sculpted body, her breath hitched and she lost her words. She scrambled for purchase in her mind and mentally shook herself. This effect he had on her was precisely why she needed some space. She couldn't tell if the overwhelming attraction she felt for him was wiping out her sanity, or if her feelings contained the depth she felt. She needed enough distance to know.

She straightened up and set the snowbrush on the hood of her car. She removed her mittens and clapped them together, knocking the snow loose. Cam walked toward her and leaned against the back corner of her car. "Hey there. Feeling better?" he asked.

"Yeah. Just a headache. I'm fine."

He nodded, his eyes searching. His shoulders rose and fell with a breath. "Would you tell me if something was wrong?" he asked abruptly.

Her stomach tightened, and her heart skipped a beat. She was silent long enough that he continued. "Over the weekend, it seemed like...I don't know, like something was wrong. I know Ivy being here kept me busy, but..."

She shook her head. "It's not that. It was great to meet Ivy..." She paused and gulped in air. She didn't want to talk now, but he was asking questions, so she'd just get it over with. "I think we need to take a break. This is all happening so fast and I don't know what you want and I don't know what I want—I don't know if you're staying in Diamond Creek and..." Her words flew out and then suddenly stopped. She couldn't stop the fear spinning inside, or the emotions careening within her.

Cam's eyes widened and he pushed away from her car to step in front of her. "Ginger, can we..."

She cut him off. "No! I need to think. I can't think when I'm with you all the time. I have to go to work." She turned away from his eyes. She could hardly bear to look at them. She grabbed the snowbrush and opened her car door, tossing it inside. She started to climb in when he curled a hand around her arm.

"I love you," he said. "I know it's happened fast, but please don't do this. Give me a chance to talk to you. I..."

His words slammed into her. Hope soared inside, her heart clamoring to be heard over the din of her fears—those familiar fears that helped her build walls around her heart to keep them out. She couldn't do this now. It was too much, and she wasn't ready. "Cam, I can't do this. Not now. Just give me a little time. Please." She shook his hand off and climbed in her car. She couldn't keep from glancing up, and the look on his face twisted her heart. His eyes were dark with confusion and pain.

She put her car in gear and backed up. As she drove away, she glanced in her rear view mirror. Cam stood there in the snow in her driveway. With her heart heavy, her stomach queasy, and her mind a muddle of confusion, she went to work.

* * *

CAM SKIED toward the warming hut by the ski lift. He stopped beside it and stepped out of his skis. A few minutes later, he was seated on one of the benches against the walls. He took a swallow of water and leaned his head back with his sigh. He'd been skiing straight through the day. He'd doubled his usual routes through the slopes and back-country trails, checking on other skiers, helping with a few minor falls, and basically trying to ski away the pain in his heart since this morning. He'd known he and Ginger needed to talk, but she'd blindsided him this morning. He hadn't even fully adjusted to the way he felt about her, but then he'd gone and blurted out he loved her. He thought it only made things worse. Now he was stuck figuring out what to do next.

The idea that Ginger might decide she didn't want to be with him was like a knife straight to his heart. He wanted to push, to demand she look at what they had and see it for what it was. Maybe he hadn't talked about his plans, but he knew what they had was special. Between Ivy's cheerful pressure for him to find somewhere to call home and his own internal confusion, he hadn't quite been ready to make any formal decisions. The only thing he had any clarity about was the fact he couldn't imagine life without Ginger. He'd come to Last Frontier Lodge to find a way to heal the hole in his heart from his brother's death. He'd been able to find a sense of peace here. He would always miss Eric, the ache of that loss would ripple forever, but he'd gotten his footing back again. He'd found Ginger. Now, he was afraid he might lose her.

"Fuck!"

He flung his empty water bottle across the small room. It landed against the wall with a rather unsatisfying thump. Empty plastic bottles only had so much oomph. At that moment, the door swung open and Gage stepped inside, kicking the snow off his boots before he shut the door.

"Hey, man. How's it going?" Gage asked as he pulled his gloves and hat off before plunking down on the bench across from Cam.

Cam tried to marshal a smile, but it just wouldn't come. He shrugged. "Just the usual."

"Can you toss me a water?" Gage asked, nodding towards the cabinet beside Cam, which was stocked with water.

Cam reached inside and quickly tossed a bottle of water to Gage. Gage caught it with one hand and took a long swallow before he set it on the bench. "Is the usual you skiing like a madman all over the mountain, not eating lunch and avoiding everyone?" Gage asked with an arch of his brow.

Cam sighed. Gage was damn perceptive, so he didn't see any point in denying the obvious. "Sorry man. Didn't mean to be an ass. Had a rough morning."

"Wanna talk about it?"

Cam considered Gage's question. He sure as hell needed to talk about it, but he wasn't used to talking about things like feelings with other men. It didn't help that he wasn't used to having feelings like he did for Ginger. He felt like he was skiing blind in a snowstorm. He leaned his head against the wall. He didn't have anything to lose besides his pride by talking with Gage. Gage had known Ginger far longer than he had and happened to be married to Ginger's oldest and best friend.

"Ginger told me she needed a break this morning."

"Ah. I see. Did something happen?"

"Just that. I didn't see it coming. This whole thing with her took me by surprise, but I don't know what the hell to do now."

Gage took a few chugs of water and leaned back. "What do you want?"

Cam's heart skipped a beat and his stomach felt hollow. He was only starting to come to terms with how he felt about her inside himself. He doubted he'd have had the courage to tell her he loved her if it hadn't happened the way it did where he felt backed up against the moment and afraid she was slipping through his fingers. He looked over at Gage. Gage was a quiet, low-key man, but Cam knew he felt things deeply. He saw it in the way Gage looked at Marley and how he cared for his family.

"I didn't see it coming, hell I didn't plan on even thinking about a relationship. But here I am. I love her."

Gage nodded slowly. "Thought so."

"That obvious?"

Gage smiled ruefully. "Only because I've been right where you are."

"Any suggestions?"

Gage chuckled. "I don't know. You and Ginger are your own people. Did she say why she needed a break?"

"She said something about everything happening too fast and that she didn't know what I wanted, or what she wanted. Everything got fuzzy after that. I want to call her and talk, but I think she might feel like I'm pressuring her."

Gage nodded slowly. "Ginger definitely doesn't like to be pressured. I'll talk to Marley and see if she has any idea what's running through Ginger's brain, but that doesn't mean she's going to tell me. They're best friends and have been forever. I'll say this though, make sure she knows how you feel. She got burned pretty bad by her ex from what Marley told me. Trust is kind of a thing for her."

Cam sighed. "I know. How the hell do I make sure she knows how I feel when she won't even talk to me?"

"Logistics. All you have to do is call her. If she won't answer, leave a message."

"Great. I'm supposed to declare my love on a voice message? I told her I loved her this morning. Isn't that enough?"

"It's a start, but if she's worried about what you want, she needs to know if you're planning on being around. You know, those pesky details. Love is great and all, but if you're not around, then it doesn't matter too much."

Cam ran a hand through his hair and sighed. Again. "Look, I'll be wherever I need to be with her. I've been meaning to talk to you about staying on after this season anyway. I love it here. My parents aren't sure where they plan to go after they retire in a few years, so I don't have any reason to try to settle down near them right now. Ivy, well, Ivy's going to go where her research and her brains take her. Diamond Creek would be a good place for me to settle down anyway, and Ginger makes it the one and only option."

Gage grinned. "Can't say I'm not happy about that. You'd be hard to replace. With the ski classes and your reputation, we're already booking halfway into next winter. Plus, you're damn easy to work with." His eyes sobered. "Ginger needs to know you'll be around."

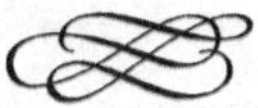

CHAPTER 19

Cam paced back and forth in front of the windows in his suite. It was day four of radio silence from Ginger. He'd tried calling her, but had yet to marshal the courage to leave her a message beyond asking her to call him. He stopped pacing and stared out into the fading light. There would be no glorious sunset over the mountains this evening. The sky had been thick with clouds all day. No snow had fallen, although the air had been scented with it all day.

His phone beeped, indicating a text had arrived. He slipped it out of his pocket, his stomach clenching when he saw Ginger's name. He tapped the message to open it.

Look, I got your messages. When I said I needed a break, I meant it. Please stop calling. I can't see you right now. I'm sorry.

Cam grabbed his jacket and slammed out of his room. With his stomach churning, he raced out of the lodge to his truck. Maybe Ginger refused to see reason, but he had to talk to her. As he climbed into his truck, his phone vibrated. He yanked it out and answered without thinking. It was his mother. He'd just spoken to her yesterday, so it was unusual for her to call again this quickly. "Hey Mom, what's up?"

"Cam, I'm sorry to call like this, but I'm at the hospital with your father."

"What?! What happened?"

"Your father collapsed at work. They called me right after they called the ambulance. I met the ambulance here, but I still haven't heard back from the doctors. The paramedics said he had a heart attack."

Cam's heart stuttered and his stomach felt queasy. He was caught between the tides of worry for his father and worry for how his mother was handling it. He batted his thoughts away and stayed focused. "Okay, okay. Have they given you any information on whether he's stable or not?"

"He's in the operating room. The paramedics told me they were able to stabilize him on the way to the hospital, but that's it."

"How're you doing, Mom?"

He could hear her take a shaky breath. "I'm okay. I'm scared, and I wish I knew what happened, but I'm okay."

"I should be able to be there soon. I'll book a flight as soon as I get off the phone. Have you called Ivy yet?"

"Honey, you don't need…"

"Mom, there's no way I'm not coming down there, so don't try to talk me out of it."

He could hear her sigh. "Okay. I'm glad you're coming. I called Ivy right before I called you, but I only got her voice mail. I asked her to call back, but I didn't want to leave a message about this."

"I'll try to call her on the way to the airport. If you're okay, I'm gonna hang up and get going. Once I know my flight schedule, I'll call again. Okay?"

"Okay. I'll let Ivy know you're on the way if I talk to her before she talks to you."

He started to say goodbye when his mother interjected. "Cam?"

"Yeah?"

"Thank you for coming down here."

"Of course, Mom. I'll see you as soon as I can get there."

Once he got off the phone, he went into action. He got out of his truck and jogged back up to his room in the lodge, his probably ill advised drive to Ginger's house abandoned. With his mind bouncing between worry about his father and feeling torn up over Ginger's text, he snagged his laptop and made the earliest flight reservation he could, which gave him almost no time to spare. He threw some clothes in a backpack and ran down the back stairs to find Gage. He raced through the kitchen and into Gage's office. Gage was sitting at his desk, his eyes glued to his computer screen. He looked up when Cam came through the door.

"You okay?" Gage asked immediately.

Cam ignored the question. "I need to fly out to Utah. My mom called. Sounds like my dad might've had a heart attack, but she's not exactly sure. He's in surgery right now. Is it gonna be okay if I take off on short notice like this?"

Gage stood quickly. "Of course! You don't even need to ask. Need a ride to the airport?"

Cam glanced at the clock on the wall above the door. "Actually, that would be great. I booked a flight leaving in forty-five minutes."

Gage grabbed his jacket off the back of his chair. "Let's go."

Roughly two hours later, Cam walked off the plane onto the tarmac in Anchorage. He walked through the falling darkness, following the line of passengers into the main airport. The small regional flights from Diamond Creek landed at the gates as far away as possible from where he needed to be to catch his flight to Seattle and onward to Utah.

Once he was inside the airport, he started jogging. He made it to his gate with a few minutes to spare. He tugged his phone out and checked his messages. Ivy had called to report she was also flying in and would wait for him at the airport. His mother had left a message that his father was still in surgery.

He held his phone in his hand for a long moment before he quickly called Ginger. Even though she'd asked him to stop calling, he had to at least let her know what was going on. He needed her to know he'd be back once he knew his father was okay. Yet again, his call went to voice mail. With his heart beating like a drum in his ears, he left her a message.

Hey Ginger. I was hoping I'd have a chance to talk to you, but since I haven't, you're getting this in a message. My dad's in the hospital, so I'm flying down to Utah tonight. I'll be back as soon as I know he's okay. He paused to gulp in air. *Look, I didn't get a chance to tell you this the right way, but here goes. I know you asked me not to call, but I want to make sure you know how I feel. I'm not going anywhere. I've already talked to Gage about staying on at the lodge. I hope...I hope you'll give us a chance. I'm about to get on another plane and won't be able to talk until about two in the morning tomorrow. If you want me to call, leave a message and I'll call as soon as I can. I, uh, I love you.*

His flight was announced for boarding the second he hung up.

* * *

"Dammit!"

Ginger threw her phone across the room where it fortunately landed on the couch with a thump. Cam had left her a message. She'd been desperate to talk to him for days and nearly at war with herself over what to do. Weary of feeling so vulnerable and partly angry with him for mattering so much to her, she'd sent that damn text telling him not to call. For a brief time, she'd felt relieved. She'd felt like she was taking control of her life again. Then last night, she'd almost lost it. She felt like a coward and was terrified she was pushing too hard. Her pride had kept her from calling him because she didn't know how to move past her own stubbornness.

Now, he'd gone and called her anyway. Wherever he'd called from, the reception was crap. She'd only gotten bits and pieces. He was on his way to Utah because of something to do with his dad. He'd be back and he loved her. She had more questions than answers. She grabbed her phone and tried to call him back, but it went straight to voice mail. Her throat was tight and hot tears pressed against the back of her eyes. She swung from desperately wanting to talk to Cam to pushing back against the feeling again. She hated how out of control she felt. While she paced back and forth in front of the woodstove, George watched her calmly from his perch on the windowsill. Impatient, she called Marley. As soon as Marley answered, Ginger started talking. "Do you know what's going on with Cam? He left me a message, but I can't hear half of it. Why is he going to Utah and…"

"Slow down! I can barely keep up," Marley interjected. "I'll answer what I can. Cam's dad is in the hospital, so he flew down there last night. Gage dropped him off at the airport. His flights through Seattle and onto Utah were during the night, so we haven't had an update yet. My guess is he went straight to the hospital. Gage said Ivy was meeting him there. That's all I know."

Ginger stopped pacing and flung herself on the couch with a heavy sigh. "Do you know if his dad's okay?" Her heart ached with worry for Cam and for his father. He'd already had too much loss to absorb with his brother's death.

"When Gage dropped him off last night, the latest update was Cam's dad was in surgery. We haven't heard anything this morning, but like I said he flew through the night and probably went straight to the hospital. Have you tried calling him?"

Ginger sighed impatiently. "Yes! That's why I'm calling you. His phone went straight to voice mail."

"Okay. Why don't you come up here for breakfast?" Marley asked, her voice soft.

"I have to go to work." Ginger twisted her hair around her finger and chewed on her lip.

"You don't have to go to work. It's completely okay for you to call out. Your boyfriend's father is in the hospital. You're not going to be much use at work anyway. I'll come pick you up," Marley said, her tone firm.

Ginger's brain got hung up on the word 'boyfriend.' Cam, her boyfriend? Oddly enough, the word seemed too important and too insignificant at the same time. She knew Marley was right. She was different now—emotionally alive. Her feelings for Cam were raw, charged and over-whelming—and impossible to ignore.

"Okay. I'll come up in a bit. You don't need to come get me though."

After she hung up, she tried to call Cam again only to get his voice mail again. This time, she left a message.

Hey. It's me. I got your message. I didn't catch everything because the connection was spotty, but Marley filled in some of the blanks. I hope your dad's okay. I'm, uh, I'm thinking about you.

She hung up abruptly. She wanted to tell him she loved him, but she couldn't seem to form the words. Why did she have to go and fall in love with a man who made her stumble over her words? As soon as that thought crossed her brain, the tears welled up inside again. This, all of this, was why she'd thought it was best never to let anyone matter too much again. All she was trying to do was get some perspective on how she felt about Cam and she was nearly falling apart because of it. Throw in what was happening with his father, and her heart ached with worry.

She ran upstairs and showered and dressed in record time. While she was making coffee and getting fresh food out for George, she called her work. The school secretary sounded completely startled to learn Ginger was calling out for the day. After Ginger hung up, she couldn't help but laugh. In three years, this was the first time she'd called out from work. She'd gone to work rain or shine and even when she was sick. It took her losing her mind over a man to make her feel like she couldn't handle work.

Her stomach flipped in a slow circle. A rush of vulnerability washed through her. She couldn't allow herself to dwell and grabbed her jacket and purse before dashing out the door. She zoomed up to the lodge. She checked her phone to see if she'd missed a call from Cam when she got to the lodge, but her screen was blank.

Hours later, she was pacing back and forth in Marley and Gage's living room. "Why hasn't he called me back? Do you think his dad's okay?"

Marley had just returned to the living room from putting Holly down for a nap. She brushed her auburn hair back with her hands and quickly tied it in a knot before sitting down on the couch.

"Well?" Ginger asked impatiently, throwing her hands up before stopping a few feet in front of where Marley was seated.

"How in the world am I supposed to be able to answer those questions?"

"I don't know. I just...I just want to know what's going on."

"I know," Marley said softly. "I hate to tell you, but I think you might have to accept that you need to wait. You've called him and left him a few messages. He could be tied up at the hospital, or maybe he doesn't have good reception there. You know how those giant buildings are. Sit down." She patted the couch.

Ginger sighed heavily and threw herself on the couch. At that moment, there was a quick knock on the door. Marley called out for whomever it was to come in. Delia stepped through the door. She glanced between Marley and Ginger and immediately walked to the couch, sitting down at an angle across from Ginger. Her eyes were warm as she looked over.

"Any news?" she asked without preamble. Marley had briefed her earlier when Ginger arrived at the lodge.

Ginger shook her head and tried to quell the anxiety coursing through her in waves. She'd been battling her internal unease all morning. It was now late morning, and she hadn't heard a word from Cam. She considered that she'd demanded he give her space and now she felt horrible about it. She hadn't thought about what it would feel like to want to talk to someone and not be able to. She'd done it without even considering how he might feel. She *had* needed the space, but maybe she could have tried to talk with him more instead of ignoring the phone every time he called for four days straight.

She rolled her head to the side and looked from Marley to Delia. "I suck at waiting," she said with a sigh.

Marley laughed softly. "Yeah, you do. Well, only for some things. You're super patient with kids and…"

"And nothing and nobody else," Ginger interjected. She realized her impatience with herself and Cam was what led her to shut him out. She didn't even have patience to wait and see how things unfolded.

Marley shrugged. "So what? We can't all be patient. Anyway, my point was you can spend all day pacing and freaking out, or you can accept there's not much you can do."

Delia chimed in. "Or you could do something about it," she said firmly.

"Like what?"

Delia pursed her lips and angled her head to the side. "You might need to start by actually admitting how much Cam means to you."

Ginger's stomach flipped and her throat tightened with emotion again. She swallowed and gulped in air. "What do you mean?"

Delia arched a brow, but remained silent. When Ginger glanced to Marley, she merely shrugged.

Feeling obstinate, Ginger rolled her eyes. "Fine. I love him. You know as well as I do that love doesn't mean every-thing works out."

Marley's brows hitched up and her eyes widened before she shook her head. Delia threw her hands up. "Oh my God! Now you're just being stubborn. If you're referring to your first marriage, that doesn't even count. You didn't love Tony. Maybe you thought you did, but you didn't. Tony sure as hell didn't love you. You love Cam and that's different." Delia's voice softened. "And Cam loves you."

Delia's words hit Ginger right in her heart. Her heart gave a hard kick and that anxious feeling rose up again.

Delia kept talking. "Don't let a good thing go just because you're scared."

Marley nodded firmly. Ginger looked between them and almost laughed. She had bossy friends, but she was the same kind of friend to them, so she got it. Their bossy support right now eased her anxiety. She took a breath and let it out slowly. "I guess I'm kind of freaking out. I feel so out of control, like I can't get a handle on anything."

"Yeah, well, this part of falling in love is kind of like that," Marley offered with a rueful grin.

Delia leaned back against the couch. "I wouldn't be saying any of this if it wasn't so obvious how you two feel about each other. I get the whole trust thing. Remember, Nick's father wasn't exactly a great guy. But when you find the right man, it's worth it."

Ginger looked out the windows. The wind was blowing the snow off the spruce boughs. Her stomach fluttered and her heart raced. She didn't know if she was crazy, but she just wanted to be with Cam. She wanted to make sure he was okay and knew she was there for him if he needed her. *Um, if you're going to go down there, you might want to get up the nerve to tell him how you feel.* She started to swat the thought away and then realized it was pointless. She loved Cam and she had to make sure he knew.

She stood up swiftly. "I'm going down there. Will one of you take care of George?"

"Of course. I'll bring him up here," Marley said quickly. "That way he won't be alone while you're gone. Do you need a ride to the airport?"

"First, I have to make reservations."

Marley leaned over and grabbed her laptop off the coffee table. "Let's do it right now. If you fly out of Diamond Creek, it's a puddle jumper flight. You don't mind those, right?"

"Nah. Just book me on the quickest flight."

CHAPTER 20

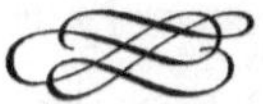

Cam returned to the waiting room with two cups of hospital coffee in hand. His mother was napping in a corner chair, while Ivy sat nearby typing away on her laptop as usual. He sat down beside Ivy and set a cup of coffee on the table beside her. "Here you go. It might not be the best, but it's definitely caffeinated."

Ivy looked up and closed her laptop, snatching the coffee and taking a big gulp. "It's not too bad," she said with a grin.

Cam shrugged. "So, so. You don't have to stop working because I'm here."

"I was just getting through some emails." She reached over and squeezed his hand quickly. "I'm glad you came. Mom's fine either way, but it means a lot to her to have you here."

"I know. Just like it means a lot to her for you to be here." He paused and took a swallow of coffee, savoring the bitter flavor. "You know, once we know a little more about dad, maybe we should talk with mom and dad about him backing off work some. They keep talking about retiring every so often, but maybe it's time to push things along."

Ivy's eyes were somber. "Maybe so. Let's get to the part where we know a little more about how he's doing first, okay?"

He leaned back in his chair. "Sure. Just putting it out there." When they'd arrived early this morning, their father had gotten out of surgery and they were told it would be another two to three hours before they could see him. He was reportedly in the recovery room and would then be transferred to ICU. Cam was tired and his emotions were unsteady. His mind swung between worrying about his father, how his mother was coping, and wondering if Ginger had gotten his message.

As if on cue, Ivy asked, "Have you heard from Ginger?"

His heart clenched as he shook his head. He hadn't checked his phone since this morning after he and Ivy arrived at the hospital. He'd gotten weary of checking it and having his hopes dashed again and again. Though he knew it was probably pointless, he fumbled in his pocket and pulled his phone out. "Aw, fuck. My battery died. You happen to have a charger with you? I didn't even think to bring mine. I was in such a rush when I left."

Ivy grinned. "I'm a computer geek. Of course I have a charger!" She dug through her backpack and tossed a charger over to him. He quickly plugged his phone in. He and Ivy were quietly nursing their coffees when the doctor came into the waiting room. Cam stood quickly. "Any updates, Dr. Martin?"

Ivy scrambled out of her chair and went to gently nudge their mother's shoulder. "Hey Mom, the doctor's here with an update."

The doctor walked across the waiting room and sat down in the chair beside their mother once she was awake. "Your husband's going to be okay, April. Like I said earlier, he had a heart attack, but his vital signs are still stable. He'll remain in ICU for another three or four days."

Cam's mother, April Nash, was a librarian, so she approached everything with methodical, logical questions. Since he and Ivy had arrived during the night at the hospital, April had been emotional, but calm. She immediately started asking the doctor questions.

"When can we see him?"

Dr. Martin smiled. "That's why I'm here. He can have visitors in about a half hour, but only one at a time and only for a few minutes."

His mother nodded quickly. Her brown eyes were tired and worried. She looked between Cam and Ivy before turning back to the doctor. "Can you explain how his surgery went?"

Dr. Martin nodded. "He had open-heart surgery. His heart attack occurred because his left anterior descending artery was almost completely blocked. It's fortunate someone was with him when it occurred because he arrived at the hospital within minutes. I need to be honest and tell you survival rates from the kind of heart attack your husband had are not good if the person doesn't receive prompt surgical intervention. Fortunately, we were able to clear the blockage and place a stent in the artery. Once he's able to participate in planning, we'll need to talk about monitoring the stent and making sure he routinely sees a cardiologist."

Cam's mother nodded along and continued asking questions, while Cam's thoughts spun wild. He was no medical expert, but by chance he knew what it meant for someone to have a blockage in the left anterior descending artery. Those heart attacks were called 'widow makers' because of how deadly they were. His father had survived, but he would need to be vigilant going forward. Cam glanced to Ivy whose eyes held the same worry her felt.

Dr. Martin stood and glanced to Cam and Ivy. "Do either of you have any questions for me?"

When they shook their heads in unison, he nodded. "Feel free to page me if you do. A nurse will be down shortly to let you know when you can visit your father."

At that, Dr. Martin turned and walked away. Cam and Ivy sat down on opposite sides of their mother. Cam looked at his mother. She tucked her brown hair behind her eyes and met his gaze. "I'm fine. You don't need to keep asking me how I'm doing," she said firmly.

Cam sighed and ran his hands through his hair. "It would be okay if you weren't fine, Mom."

April smiled ruefully. "I know it would. I had some long hours last night where I had a rough patch, but your father's going to be okay. You just heard Dr. Martin say he would. His recovery will take some time, but he's okay and that's all that matters."

Ivy hooked her hand in her mother's elbow. "That is all that matters. We just want you to know you don't have to be strong for us. If you need someone to lean on, we're both here."

April looked from Ivy to Cam and smiled. "I know you are."

A WHILE LATER, Cam stood by his father's bed. His father was asleep. His mother had visited first and then Ivy. The nurses had explained his father would only come in and out of consciousness due to the lingering effects of the anesthesia after a six-hour surgery. Cam's eyes traveled over the tubes hooked up to his father. Eric Nash, Sr. was a stately looking man, even when he looked vulnerable in his hospital bed. His hair had faded to gray and, at the moment, his skin had a grayish hue. Cam's heart felt heavy. He was beyond relieved it looked like his father would be okay, but this scare was significant. When he'd mentioned to Ivy they might want to talk with their parents about planning, it hadn't quite sunk in for him how serious his father's heart attack had been.

The sliding doors into his father's ICU room opened, and a nurse poked her head through the door. "Another minute, okay?"

Cam nodded and stood up. He curled his hand around his father's, which lay limply on the edge of the bed. He gave it a quick squeeze. "Love you, Dad," he whispered before he stepped away and quietly left the room. He walked down the hall to a small alcove where a vending machine held snacks, along with an automated coffee maker. He fed a dollar bill in the coffee machine and waited for the beep to indicate his coffee cup was full. He added a dash of creamer and headed back to the waiting room.

He rounded the corner and almost choked on the sip of coffee he'd just taken. Ginger stood beside Ivy. She turned toward the doorway when he stepped into the room. Her dark hair was mussed, and her blue eyes looked worried. They stood frozen and stared at each other. Ivy hurried out of the room, glancing over her shoulder when she reached the door. "I'll be in the cafeteria with Mom."

Cam's heart hammered against his ribs. Ginger tucked a loose lock of hair behind her ear. "I left you a few messages, but when I didn't hear back, I got worried. So…I decided to come down here. I hope it's okay. Ivy told me your father's okay."

Cam nodded and took a step in her direction. He wanted to wrap her in his arms and just hold on. She'd stunned him by showing up here, but he didn't know what she wanted. It occurred to him that he hadn't even checked his phone since he plugged it in for charging a while ago. He'd forgotten all about it. The long night had fogged his thoughts. All the feelings that had been tumbling through his heart in the days since Ginger asked for a break had come into sharp focus during the hours of his flight down here. He loved Ginger and all he wanted was a chance to be with her. Yet, he didn't think he could do anything with her in half-measures. He could wait, but he couldn't try to fumble along if he didn't know where she stood. To see her here, in the antiseptic environment of the hospital while he felt worn, weary and could most definitely use a shower, wasn't ideal—not when his heart longed to pull her close and hold her.

Ginger bit her lip and clasped and unclasped her hands in front of her. "Cam, I'm, uh, I'm sorry I shut you out like that. I just..." She paused and crossed her arms over her chest. "I'm sorry. Maybe now isn't the best time to talk. I didn't come here to make this all about me. I just wanted to be here for you. How are you?"

"I'm fine. It's been a long night, but my dad's gonna be okay. That's all I could ask for." He paused and took a gulp of coffee, trying to gather his frayed nerves. Her eyes coasted over him, but she was quiet. He needed to know what she'd meant to say when she first started talking. "Now's a good time to talk," he said, his voice coming out gruff.

She looked puzzled. "What do you mean?"

He took another swallow of coffee. He needed the caffeine to keep his brain functioning. His heart was still pounding and anxiety was coiling in his stomach. With his emotions bouncing all over the place, he was grasping for an anchor inside, but he was coming up short. "You started to say something and then said you didn't come here to make it about you. My dad's okay, so I'm okay. I want to hear what you were about to tell me."

"Oh." One word and then silence hung in the room. He felt it with every beat of his heart, but he waited.

* * *

GINGER'S PULSE raced madly and her stomach clenched with anxiety. She'd flown down here, her thoughts clouded with worry, driven only by the urge to be by Cam's side and make sure he was okay. He stood across from her in the hospital waiting room. The walls were a soft cream color and the chairs varying pastel shades, everything intended to be soothing and unobtrusive. Inside, she was a wild mess—her feelings swirling madly. Cam wanted her to finish what she'd meant to say and fear clogged her throat. She was nearly torn inside between desperately wanting to fling her arms around him and tell him she loved him and wanting to turn and run away. Her feelings were too big, too encompassing. His broken message had left too many gaps for her to feel the certainty she craved.

She looked over at him. His golden-brown hair glinted under the bright hospital lights. His amber eyes were fatigued, yet they held her fast in his intent gaze. Something settled within her. She couldn't wait for guarantees. If Cam had the courage to tell her he loved her without knowing how she felt, she could at least return the favor—especially since he'd already offered her the gift of his feelings. Her heart, or perhaps her guarded, slightly cynical mind, wanted a certainty that life didn't offer, so she had to take the chance. She took a breath and dredged up her courage.

"I meant to say I'm sorry for how I handled things the other day." She paused for a breath and to consider how to explain herself to him. It occurred to her it had been a mere four days ago when he'd stood in the snow by her car and told her he loved her. It felt like eons had passed because she'd missed him so. The worn grooves of worry and rumination in her mind seemed just that—worn. The walls she'd put up around her heart had gotten in her way with Cam. While his love may not come with guarantees, no one's did and she knew he would never hurt her on purpose. "I got scared because you matter so much to me. I love you. It scared me because I never meant to love anyone again. With you, it's so much more than I ever imagined. I'm not making excuses, but I want you to understand why I…well, why I freaked out. I did need a little space to get my head on straight, but I wish I'd just talked to you instead of shutting you out."

Her words ran out, along with her breath. She gulped in air and twisted her hands together. Cam stood there for so long she was afraid she'd misunderstood. Maybe he didn't really love her, maybe he said the words in an impulsive, overwrought moment. He moved, slowly and deliberately, and set his coffee down on a small table by the chairs. In two quick strides, he was in front of her. His hands came to rest on her shoulders and she looked up. What she saw in his eyes made her heart soar and hope spin in wild circles.

One hand stroked up into her hair, curling around the nape of her neck, while the other stroked down her back. The heat of his palm sent a jolt of electricity racing up her spine. He dipped his head slowly, his forehead coming to rest against hers. "So are you done needing space?" he asked, his voice sending a shiver through her.

"Yes," she managed to reply, her voice barely a whisper. "I didn't mean…"

"It's okay. I understand. You had your reasons to worry. Maybe I didn't have the same ones, but I get it."

His lips were so close, she could feel them moving against hers. Her body flexed toward him, drawn solely by the force between them. She sighed with relief when his lips caught hers. His kiss started soft, but in seconds, she lost all sense of time and place. She felt starved for his touch. He fit his mouth over hers and swept his tongue into her mouth, stroking against hers. Heat blazed through her, and she gasped when his palm slid down to cup her bottom. Suddenly, he tore his mouth away.

"Dammit," he whispered roughly. "You make me crazy, but we have to stop before I forget where we are."

He dropped his forehead to her shoulder and took a shuddering breath. "I love you, you know." His words were muffled against her skin. Her heart clenched and opened.

"I love you too."

He lifted his head and stroked her hair away from her face. His eyes were warm, and she felt hot tears at the back of hers.

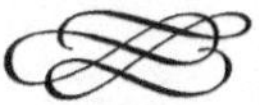

CHAPTER 21

Cam slung his bag over his shoulder and walked out of the guest room at his parents' house. Ginger had flown back to Diamond Creek two days ago after staying with him in Utah for over a week. His father had been discharged from the hospital three days ago. He and Ivy had stayed to make sure everything was settled, his father was comfortable and his mother had everything she needed. Ivy was staying for another few days. Cam had offered, but his mother was beyond annoyed to have both of her children fussing over them.

Yesterday morning, his mother had looked across the table at him. "You need to get back to Alaska and Ginger."

"Mom, I can stay as long as…"

His mother, who was almost always polite, rolled her eyes. "I don't need anything. Your father is going to go mad with all of us hovering over him. It's been wonderful to have you here, but I'd be much happier to know you were where you want to be."

Cam had bitten back a laugh and agreed to book a flight

back to Alaska soon. This morning, he made his way down the hall to find his father in his study. His father was leaning back in a recliner he and Ivy had wrangled into the study the day before his father was discharged from the hospital. Eric, Sr. rolled his head to the side when Cam entered the room.

"Morning, Dad," Cam said as he sat down in a chair across from his father.

"Morning. I suppose you're here to find out how I'm feeling. No need to ask. I'm fine. What I am is sick and tired of everyone checking on me."

Cam chuckled. "I can see you're fine, so I'll skip asking." He paused and glanced around the room, his eyes scanning across multiple photographs of him and his brother, almost all of them somewhere in the mountains on skis. There were just as many photos of Ivy, although most of hers were of her receiving academic awards. His gaze made it back to his father. His father's eyes were similar to his and Ivy's. Right now, the amber was flashing with annoyance.

"Before I fly out this afternoon, I wanted to check in and see what your plans are for the store. Have you thought about it much?"

His father sighed and leaned his head back. "My new cardiologist says I need to minimize stress. I love working, but the pace is too much. I'm planning to sell the store and then your mother and I will figure out what's next. I won't stop working altogether, but I'll work less. Your mother will want to stay here until she knows you and Ivy are settled."

Cam was relieved at his father's decision, but surprised he'd made it so quickly. "Well, I'm glad to hear you're planning to sell the store, but…"

"You can't believe I'm letting go that fast?" his father asked with a chuckle.

"That's what I was going to say. Do you feel okay about it?"

His father shrugged. "Your mother and I had already talked about it. I'm not as young as I used to be, and this year's been hard on both of us. I knew I needed to slow down, but it's amazing the perspective you can get from almost dying. I'll never like being hovered over. I won't be good at sitting around, but I don't have to work so hard, so I can be sensible."

Cam nodded and swallowed at the emotion tightening in his chest. His father had made it through this scare all in one piece, but hearing him say so plainly that he'd almost died was sobering. After another breath, Cam glanced over. "All right then. I won't hover, but you'd better be ready for me to visit more often."

His father grinned. "I like Ginger. She's good for you. I'm glad you stopped in one place long enough to find her. Alaska's not too far from here. After all your traveling, we'll see lots more of you now. Especially since we have somewhere to visit you. That's new."

"I guess I hadn't thought of it like that."

His father adjusted the recliner and slowly stood. "Let's go have breakfast. Your mother won't let me hear the end of it if you don't sit down with us before you go."

* * *

AN ICY GUST blew Ginger's hood back, and she tugged it back up as she ran across the parking lot at the airport. Cam's flight had just landed. She'd waited in her car and watched the small plane come in for a landing. The plane had wobbled in the wind, but landed safely. The few passengers were climbing out and waiting while the pilot pulled their bags out of the small hold under the plane. Ginger waited by the gate. Diamond Creek's airport was tiny. The small building housed a counter where the sole airline that flew in here and a car rental place shared the space.

The 'gate' was a door where passengers came in and out to walk to the small six-seater planes. Cam snagged his bag from the pilot and strode quickly to the door. As soon as he stepped inside, his eyes landed on Ginger. Her pulse rocketed and heat washed through her. All he had to do was look and her body went wild. She ran to meet him and didn't even stop to think when she threw her arms around him. His bag thudded to the floor as he wrapped both arms around her. His lips met hers in swift kiss.

When he pulled away, he was smiling. "Damn, it's good to see you."

"It's only been two days," she replied, unable to keep from smiling. It had only been two days, but two days felt like forever. His arms loosened, and she slid to the floor. "Let's go. It's freezing out."

Cam picked up his bag and walked at her side, her hand held in the warm grip of his. Once they were in the car, he glanced to her. "Your place?"

"You sure you don't want to stop by the lodge first?"

He shook his head firmly. "The only person I want to see tonight is you."

His words sent a hot thrill through her. Though they'd just spent the last week together, they'd had hardly a moment alone. She nodded and started driving. By the time, she pulled up at her house, Cam had nearly driven her wild by curling his palm over her thigh and stroking his thumb back and forth slowly. She was drenched with need and heat suffused her entire body. Somehow, she managed to get out of the car. The contrast of the icy air to the heat inside temporarily eased the desire pounding through her.

It was late afternoon, the sky was gray and the air was scented with snow. The water in the bay was choppy from the wind. Once they were inside, they hung their jackets and kicked their shoes off. She went straight to the woodstove. She could barely focus, so intent was Cam's presence. She needed a moment to gather herself, and the activity of laying logs in the woodstove and starting a fire grounded her slightly. When she stood, she saw Cam standing by the windows. He turned to face her. It felt as if a flame lit the air between them. He walked slowly to her. In slow motion, he lifted a hand and traced her lips. Her breath came out in a whoosh. The heat that had barely cooled in the few moments outside blazed back to life.

The pad of his thumb dented her bottom lip. Her low belly clenched. His thumb dragged down her neck, leaving her skin nearly aflame where he touched. He dipped his head, his lips following behind his fingers—a hot, wet path along her collarbone and dipping into the vee of her blouse. He methodically unbuttoned her blouse, the brush of his fingers against her abdomen leaving her trembling. By the time he lifted his head, she couldn't contain the need coursing through her. She was steaming inside and out. A bead of perspiration rolled between her breasts. He caught it with his tongue, eliciting a low moan from her. She yanked on the hem of his jersey shirt and shoved it up. Cam reached a hand behind his neck and lifted his shirt off in one move. Everything became a blur—clothes were tossed haphazardly. All she knew was the feel of Cam's hands on her, his lips and tongue mapping her body, and the feel of his hard, muscled body under her touch.

Awareness filtered into her consciousness when he lifted her against him and slowly sat down on the couch. She straddled his hips. The heated length of his cock rested against her slick folds. She couldn't resist rolling her hips. Spikes of pleasure scored through her. Feverish with need, she arched back and cried out as she slid across the hard heat of his shaft.

"Ginger."

Cam whispered her name, his words rough with desire.

She dragged her eyes open to find his molten amber gaze on her. Shivering heat licked down her spine as he dragged a finger slowly down her back. She couldn't look away—his eyes reflected her own intense need back to her. A rush of intimacy caught her and held her. He gripped her hips and shifted against her.

"Cam..."

His name fell from her lips on a breath.

"Love you."

Cam's words came just as he surged into her. He held still for a long moment. She could barely speak over the thundering of her heart. *"Love you."* Those two words were all she could manage. Skin to skin, held against him, she felt fragile and sexy and strong at once. His lips caught hers in a fierce kiss. When he slowly pulled back, she met his eyes and the flames licked higher inside, engulfing her as they started to move. She lost herself in the sensations teeming with her—the pull and slide of him within her as she rolled her hips to meet his again and again.

Each surge brought him deeper and deeper. Pleasure built and built within, the pressure gathering in a wild storm inside. Her core drew tight and a quick stroke of his thumb against her clit sent pleasure spiraling loose through her body. Her release was so intense, she collapsed against him as he went rigid underneath her and called her name roughly. His arms caught her and held her fast against him. Her head fell into the dip of his shoulder. As she slowly caught her breath, she lifted it to find his had fallen back against the couch. He opened his eyes and rolled his head to the side. A smile curled her lips with his following. Joy fluttered within her.

* * *

CAM LEANED FORWARD and set his empty plate on the coffee table. After they'd managed to untangle themselves and shower, Ginger had declared they were ordering pizza for dinner. He was now sated in more ways than one. Snow had begun to fall and was blowing sideways outside the windows, illuminated from the light inside the house. With a fire snapping in the woodstove and Ginger nibbling on a piece of pizza beside him, Cam couldn't imagine anywhere else he'd rather be. He heard the distinctive thump of George hopping across the floor and grinned.

"He can't sneak up on anyone, can he?" Cam asked.

Ginger shrugged. "Maybe not. George hasn't had the life he would've in the wild, so he doesn't have to worry about being quiet so he doesn't get eaten."

George bounced onto the couch and settled himself against Cam's leg. Cam stroked his hand over George's head and glanced to Ginger. "I forgot to ask if you could give me a ride up to the lodge tomorrow morning."

"I planned on it. I have to be at work by eight, so we just need to leave in time for me to make it back to town."

"Works for me. I'm up early whether I want to be or not."

Hours later, Cam woke during the night when a gust of wind rattled the windows. Ginger was curled up beside him, her head tucked against his shoulder and her legs tangled with his. He rolled his head to the side and looked out the windows into the dark night. The snow had stopped, but the wind was coming in gusts off the water. Stars were bright in the inky sky and the moon hung low over the mountains. Ginger shifted against him. He stroked a palm down the curve of her hip. His body tightened and he chuckled to himself. His desire for her ran unchecked. The feel of her silky skin under his touch was all his body needed to want more of her. He glanced down at her. In sleep, she was relaxed, her features soft. His heart clenched and then softened. He'd come to Alaska to find peace, which he had, but what he'd found with Ginger was worth so much more. He took a deep breath and closed his eyes. With her body warm against his, he fell back to sleep.

EPILOGUE

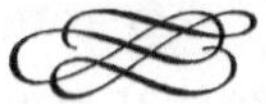

Cam tossed his cards down and arched a brow at
Gage. "I fold. My hand's crap."

Gage shrugged and played a card. Garrett instantly laid
his cards down. "Straight flush." His eyes bounced between
Cam and Gage before a slow grin spread across his face.

Gage chuckled and slowly gathered the cards off the
table and shuffled the deck before setting it down. "Okay,
you've won twice." He glanced to Cam. "Garrett's on a roll.
Unless you want to keep losing, I'd say we're done for now.
When he's hot, he's hot."

Garrett threw his head back with a laugh. "Aw, come on.
Are we quitting that soon?"

Cam grinned and nodded. "Hey, you got two games out
of us. Take what you can get."

He and Ginger were at the lodge for dinner and their
usual gathering with friends. He glanced over to see Ginger
at the corner booth by the kitchen, deep in conversation
with Marley and Delia. Her dark hair fell in tousled waves
around her shoulders and her hands were moving animat-
edly as she spoke. His heart clenched and a sense of warmth

stole through him. He and Ginger had married a few months ago, almost precisely a year after she'd landed at his feet in the snow. She'd wanted a small, intimate wedding, which was perfectly fine with Cam. All he wanted was to be with Ginger.

Gage and Garrett were bantering about something. Cam stood up and walked over to Ginger, sliding into the booth beside her. He slipped his arm around her waist and dipped his head to drop a kiss at that sweet spot he loved—where her neck curved to meet her shoulder, a place where her skin was always soft. When he lifted his head, he saw her pulse fluttering in her neck. Her cheeks were flushed, and her blue eyes were dark. She took a breath and let it out in a soft huff.

Marley chuckled softly. "Well, we don't need to wonder if you're still gaga over Ginger," she said wryly.

Cam shrugged, entirely unabashed. He didn't care who knew it. He was more than gaga over Ginger. She held his heart in her hands. The heat between them blazed so hot and fast, he couldn't imagine it ever waning. He felt the rise and fall of Ginger's breath when she gulped in air. She glanced up at him, appearing to have gathered herself.

Her eyes bounced from him to Marley and back again. "Cam likes public displays of affection. No matter how many times I tell him a little privacy isn't a bad thing."

He was surprised she didn't wag her finger at him. He gave her hip a squeeze and leaned back against the booth. "Garrett won twice, so we're done with poker for the night."

Delia rolled her eyes. "Oh God. He'll brag about it later. He loves beating Gage at cards. Says it's because he used to lose all the time when they were growing up."

Conversation carried on around him while Cam soaked in the moment. He was with the woman he loved who he happened upon in one of the most beautiful places in the world. He'd found far more than he'd ever have hoped for when he came to Last Frontier Lodge. He'd been able to find the peace he sought after his brother's death, he'd found a love he hadn't expected, and he'd found a home and community.

A balled up napkin bounced again his shoulder. "What the...?" he began to ask when his eyes landed on Garrett who was approaching them.

Garrett grinned. "You were spacing out. Just making sure you're still with us."

Cam shook his head and tossed the napkin back at Garrett. A while later, he and Ginger walked out of the lodge into the winter darkness. He paused at the foot of the stairs and looked ahead. The night sky stretched out in front of them, the stars glittering bright in the cold night air. A half moon was high above the mountains across the bay, its light shimmering on the water below. He glanced down at Ginger just when she looked up. His heart clenched and that familiar longing rolled through him. He dipped his head to drop a kiss on her lips.

* * *

GINGER WOKE with the warmth of the sun on her face. She opened her eyes and looked out the windows by the bed. The sun had just crested behind the mountains. Its light struck sparks on the surface of the bay. Cam was spooned behind her, his palm resting on her abdomen. She closed her eyes for another moment and savored his warm embrace. For the first few months after they were really together, she'd struggled with doubts and worried the rightness she felt with him would fade and surely he would come to his senses and politely depart her life. He most emphatically hadn't, and she'd finally eased into the comfort she felt with him.

She took a deep breath and opened her eyes again. His

hand shifted and slid over the curve of her hip. She felt his muscles tighten into a shivering stretch before he relaxed against her. "Good morning," he said, his voice husky with sleep. His words were muffled against her hair.

She rolled over in his arms and grinned when he opened his eyes. He was an early riser, but tended to be half-awake until he had at least one cup of coffee in him. "Good morning," she replied, running a hand through his ruffled hair. "Coffee and pancakes?"

Not much later, they were seated on the couch in the living room. Two empty plates sat on the coffee table, and Cam was nursing his second cup of coffee. George hopped onto the coffee table and sniffed curiously at the plates before bouncing off the far side of the table and onto the windowsill.

"What are we doing today?" Cam asked. He held his coffee in one hand while his other arm was stretched across the back of the couch with his hand idly sifting through her hair.

She looked out the window. The sunny morning had blown away with wind and heavy, gray clouds. Snow was on the way. She looked back at Cam. "Let's make a grocery run and come home. It looks like a storm is coming. I'd like to be settled in front of the fire before that happens."

"Sounds good."

Later that evening, the snow was blowing wild in the wind. The power had gone out hours ago. The room was lit by the glow of candles. Ginger leaned back with a grin when Cam played a winning hand. He'd stopped letting her win every card game a while ago. They kept a tally, and each week whoever lost the most games had to cook the other one dinner. She was definitely on track to make dinner next. She gathered the cards and set them on the coffee table before closing the distance between them and climbing on Cam's lap.

"Are we sleeping down here tonight?" she asked.

His lips were so close, she could feel them move when he answered. "Unless we want to freeze upstairs." With that, he caught her lips in a kiss.

* * *

Thank you for reading Falling Fast - I hope you loved Ginger & Cam's story!

For more steamy, small town romance, Jessa & Eli's story is next in Stay With Me. A fender bender lands Jessa Hamilton in the path of rugged & sexy Eli Brooks. "…sizzling, raw and readable. The characters pop off the page." Don't miss Eli's story!

Keep reading for a sneak peek!

Be sure to sign up for my newsletter for the latest news, teasers & more! Click here to sign up: http:// jhcroixauthor.com/subscribe/

Chapter 1

Jessa Hamilton stared at the photo in her hand and swallowed against the tightness in her throat. She kept pulling this photo out and looking at it, as if she looked enough it would change. Yet, it never did. Walls blackened with smoke, charred furniture and nothing else recognizable. Only she knew the shape of the room and what had been contained within its walls. Hot tears pressed against the back of her eyes, and she took a gulp of air. Her name was called, and she quickly slipped the photo in her purse and stood. She walked up to the small pick-up counter and grabbed the coffee with her name on it. Once she sat back down at her table, she took a sip and glanced out the windows. The view here was simply breathtaking—a picturesque bay sparkled under the sun with mountains rising tall on the far side. A glacier lay in a valley between two peaks, glowing translucent blue and almost mesmerizing her. The sheer beauty took her mind off the reasons behind her visit.

After a few more minutes of coffee and soaking in the view, Jessa felt able to drive the last leg of her journey. She slung her purse over her shoulder and walked outside, her coffee cup warm in her hand. It was early spring in Diamond Creek, Alaska and the air had a definite chill to it. Her small blue truck was waiting for her. She climbed in and sighed. Right now, this truck was the closest thing she had to a home. It held everything she owned, which at this point was the clothes she wore, a small bag of clothing, and a toolbox that contained her beloved paintbrushes and art supplies. She ran her good hand over the dashboard and gave it a loving pat. "Okay Blue, we've got about fifteen more minutes and then you can take a break for a while."

She started the engine and put the truck in gear. She had to maneuver carefully with her left hand, which had been injured in the same fire that burned up the apartment she left behind. With a quick glance behind her, she started to back up when she felt a thump. She whipped her head further back and saw a black truck to the far corner of her line of sight. "Oh hell. Really? Did I really just back into someone?" she asked no one, unless she could count Blue as a conversation partner. She took a deep breath and rolled the truck forward before putting it back in park. Another deep breath and she climbed out, prepared to face the music of an irate driver. She prayed she'd left nothing more than a small dent in the other truck.

When she walked to the back of her truck, she saw a man leaning against the corner of the black truck and immediately lost the ability to breathe. The man in question had dark brown hair and green eyes that locked onto her the moment she looked up at him. He wore a denim jacket over a navy blue t-shirt and faded jeans that were so worn the soft fabric molded over his muscled thighs. A pair of scuffed brown leather boots completed the ensemble. His shoulders filled out his jacket, and she caught a glimpse of his muscled chest and abs in the gap where his jacket hung open. His thumb was hooked in a pocket. Her brain fuzzed and her pulse galloped. Her lungs suddenly took over and she managed to gulp in some air.

"Hi, um, I think I backed into you. I'm really sorry. I thought I looked, but I obviously didn't look enough. Is there any damage? Let me get my insurance card and..."

The man pushed away from the truck, shaking his head. "No need. Your bumper took the hit," he said, gesturing to Blue's rear bumper. "My bumper's so beat up, I probably wouldn't have noticed anyway."

Her eyes seemed stuck. She just stood there and stared at him. When he arched a brow in question, she finally managed to tear her eyes away and look at her bumper. The corner of Blue's rear bumper bore a round dent. The knot of tension in her chest loosened slightly. She'd been carrying the little ball of tension for so many weeks now, she was used to it. Any easing of it was a pleasant surprise. She took a breath and looked back at the man, her pulse rocketing again when she met his green gaze.

"Well, that's not too bad. Blue can live with it," she said, gently patting the bumper.

"Blue?"

"My truck. Her name is Blue," she offered in explanation.

"If that's how you name trucks, I guess I should be calling mine Dusty," he said with a chuckle.

His eyes glanced from her truck to her. "You from Washington?"

"Good guess."

"Not a guess. Your license plate."

"Oh, right." She couldn't seem to think of what else to say, not when this way-too-sexy man had her tongue tied and her thoughts fuzzy.

"If you're planning to get that dent banged out, my friend has a mechanic shop just down the street."

Normally, she would want to get the dent taken care of, but normally she wasn't flat broke. She shrugged. "I'm not sure when I'll have a chance to do that. I'll be in town for a bit."

He nodded slowly. "Well, if you decide to get it fixed, Dan does good work. Can't miss it. It's the shop down the road, says Auto Shop outside."

"Just Auto Shop?"

"Yup. Dan keeps it simple. What brings you to Diamond Creek? Long drive from Washington. Well, long drive from just about anywhere outside of Alaska."

Jessa was doing her damnedest to get her pulse under control, but her pulse appeared to have a mind of its own. Aside from the fact that she couldn't seem to think clearly around this man, the last thing she wanted was to think about what brought her to Alaska. She took an unsteady breath and called upon her manners.

"I'm here visiting family for a bit."

"You have family here?"

"My brother, Gage Hamilton, runs Last Frontier Lodge. My other brother, Garrett, moved up here last year. He's married to Delia. I think her maiden name was Peters."

"I've only met your brothers a few times, but everyone in Diamond Creek is damn happy about the lodge being open again. I've been up there a few times to ski myself." His green eyes crinkled at the corners. "Suppose I should introduce myself. I'm Eli Brooks." He held a hand out.

Her arm moved of its own accord, lifting and placing her hand in his. His palm engulfed hers, the calloused surface and warmth sending shivers followed by heat rushing through her. Once her hand was in his, she froze again. After a long moment, too long to be polite, he slowly loosened his grip and released her palm. Another few beats passed when he spoke again.

"Don't suppose you'll tell me your name?"

Her cheeks heated. "Oh, oh, right. Jessa Hamilton." Right about now, she wouldn't have minded if a hole opened up in the ground. Cliché or not, she would have liked somewhere to fall in and hide. Eli was doing nothing other than being polite, and she could barely hold a conversation with him.

"Nice to meet you, Jessa," Eli replied with a slow smile. "If you're here for a bit, I'll probably see you around. Diamond Creek's pretty small."

Her belly fluttered and her heart gave a little kick. What the hell was going on with her? She'd backed into Eli's truck and was all but drooling on him. She realized she was about to enter into another long moment where she should say something. That's how conversation worked. One person said something, the other person listened and formulated a reply. If this were a game of tennis, she would have definitely lost with the tennis ball flying by her each time. She gathered her scrambled thoughts and forced herself to speak.

"Nice to meet you too. I'm sorry about bumping into your truck. It's been a long few days of driving. I'm glad your truck's okay."

Eli grinned. "No problem. Like I said, even if you had dented my bumper, it would have been joining a club." He stepped away and opened his truck door. "See you around," he said with a quick wave.

She watched while he drove away. A gust of wind blasted from the direction of the bay just across the street, blowing her hair wild.

* * *

Eli glanced in his rear view mirror and saw Jessa Hamilton standing in the parking lot. Her brown hair blew in a swirl around her face. He stopped where the parking lot met Main Street and watched as she brushed her hair back with one hand and turned to hurry back into her truck. She cradled one arm against her waist, and he wondered why. He pulled out of the parking lot and headed toward his shop. He was looking at the road in front of him, but all he could see in his mind's eye were Jessa's eyes. He'd never seen eyes like hers before—smoky gray with glimpses of silver.

When he was driving through the parking lot and saw her start to back up, he didn't have enough time to stop. For a flash, he was irritated as hell. Spring was the busiest time of year for him. Owning his own business was great, except for the fact that he only had himself to count on sometimes. He owned Game to Fish, a retail store and guiding business for the hordes of wilderness travelers that descended on Diamond Creek once the snow melted. Spring meant long days of getting the store up to speed for summer and constant calls with visitors booking trips. He'd been up since way too early this morning and didn't have time to deal with a fender bender. For a split second, he considered driving on past the little blue truck that bumped into him. He'd meant it when he said he wasn't worried about his bumper, but it seemed a tad too rude to keep driving when she pulled forward and started to climb out of her truck.

One look at her chocolate brown hair with gold streaks in it, those silvery gray eyes, and her lush, curvy body, and Eli forgot that he only had a few minutes to get back to his store. Now, he had to make up the minutes he lost and gunned his truck. Within moments, he came to a jerking stop in front of his store and grabbed the small bag from the hardware store. The doorbell jangled when he walked in, and Cliff Gibson glanced up from behind the counter.

"Hey Eli, did they have the bolts we need?" Cliff asked.

Eli tossed the small bag from the hardware store to Cliff. Cliff caught it and immediately dumped the bolts on the counter. Without a word, he stepped from behind the counter and strode to the front windows to climb on the ladder there.

"Need a hand?" Eli asked, slightly bemused by Cliff. Aside from himself, Cliff was his primary employee in the retail store portion of Game to Fish. Like Eli, Cliff had been born and raised in Alaska. He knew just about everything there was to know about fishing and hunting in the area. Sometimes, Eli was amazed at how responsible Cliff was given that he'd only graduated from college a year ago.

Cliff glanced down from the ladder. "I left the bolts on the counter," he said with a grin.

Eli stepped to the counter and snagged the bolts. After he handed them over, he watched while Cliff carefully adjusted the display rack hanging from the ceiling and replaced the two broken bolts on one side. Once he was done, Cliff returned the ladder to its storage spot in the back room and immediately got back to work on ordering supplies and gear for several upcoming trips.

Eli walked into his office and looked around. His office was small and crowded. A desk and chair were tucked into the corner with two chairs on the other side of the desk. The rest of the office was filled with a jumble of fishing and hunting gear, everything from fishing rods and hunting knives to high-end outerwear. He kicked a box out of the way and sat down at his desk, quickly opening his laptop and starting to plow through emails for reservations on guided hunts. As usual, he simultaneously tapped the speaker button on his office phone and started listening to his voice mails. The first two were from customers and the third was his mother.

"Hey Eli, haven't heard from you in a while. I wanted to see how you were doing. If you get a chance, give me a call." There was a long pause. He could hear his mother take a deep breath. *"We're doing okay, just so you know. Love you."* The

recording held another deep breath from his mother before she hung up.

Eli tried to keep reading his emails, but the screen in front of him might as well have been static. He leaned back in his chair and eyed the phone. It might as well have been ticking like a bomb. He rarely spoke to his mother and hadn't spoken to his father in over a decade when he moved to Diamond Creek from Juneau. Alaska was such a part of him, he couldn't imagine living anywhere else, so he moved far enough to get some distance—literally and figuratively.

He snatched the phone up and called his mother. After several long rings, the voice mail picked up. *"Hey Mom, got your message. Doing fine here. I'll make a deposit this afternoon. Let me know a good time to call and check in with Ryan."*

He hung up and ran a hand through his hair. His mother called only once in a while, and he knew it was due to her lingering guilt over staying with his father for too many years when he was growing up. Before Eli left Juneau, he'd set his father up in an apartment and warned him to stay away from his mother and his little brother, Ryan. Eli had been determined to make sure Ryan had a more peaceful childhood than he had. He sent his mother money to make sure she and Ryan could get by. He was in a much better place than he had been when he moved away, but one thing that helped bring him peace was steering clear of the wrecking ball that was his father.

Eli shook his head sharply and forced himself to focus on work. He confirmed a few reservations and made it through the rest of his emails before walking back out front. Cliff was talking to a few early tourists and issuing temporary fishing permits for them. He glanced to Eli when he rounded the back counter.

"I'm headed to the bank and maybe a coffee run. Need anything?" Eli asked.

"Thought you were getting coffee earlier," Cliff replied with a grin.

Eli shrugged. "Forgot. How about now?"

"I'll always take coffee. Just get me whatever the house coffee is at Misty Mountain today."

"You got it. Be back in a bit."

Eli swung through the bank and transferred enough money into his mother's bank account so she could get by for a few months. Shortly thereafter, he took a welcome gulp of coffee and climbed back into his truck, tucking Cliff's coffee in the holder while he kept his in hand. As he drove down Main Street, he saw Jessa's bright blue truck at the grocery store. Without a thought passing through his brain, he found himself pulling into the parking lot and walking inside the store.

He could always find something to buy, so he grabbed a cart and started tossing groceries in as he passed through the aisles. He couldn't quite believe he was meandering through a store, hoping for an incidental encounter with a woman he'd met for a total of maybe three minutes, five tops. Yet, here he was. He was jittery with restless energy between the jolt of coffee, his mother's phone message, and this out of the blue attraction to a woman he barely knew. He practically careened around the end of an aisle, swinging his cart into the next aisle when he bumped into something, or rather someone.

"Ooomph!"

At the muffled comment, he glanced up to find Jessa standing in front of the pasta section. His cart rolled back into him. He took in a few more details this time. She wore a denim skirt over blue leggings with a fitted white t-shirt and a gray fleece jacket tied around her waist. A pair of black cowboy boots that looked beyond worn completed her attire. As his eyes traveled to her face, her amazing silver gray eyes met his. Her hair was tied in a loose knot atop her head with wispy brown curls framing her heart-shaped face.

"Oh shit! I'm sorry. I wasn't even paying attention. Are you okay?"

She cradled her left hand against her, the same one he'd noticed earlier. "I'm fine," she said quickly. "Just a little bump. My hip can take it." Her mouth hooked in a rueful smile at that.

"You sure?" he asked with a nod toward her hand.

She glanced down and back up. "Oh, you didn't hit my hand. I, uh, injured this a few weeks ago." She held it out, and he saw her hand was sporting a gauze wrap. "It's healing fine, but it seems like I'm always walking around with it pinned to my side. I don't even think about it most of the time."

All kinds of questions tumbled through his mind. He didn't know what it was about Jessa, but she made him want to know everything about her. He didn't think it was prudent to bombard her with questions, so he merely nodded. "Well, I'm glad you're okay."

She laughed softly. "You didn't hit me nearly as hard as I hit you with Blue."

He chuckled. "Yeah, but that was my truck. This was you."

One shoulder lifted in a slow shrug. "I'm fine. No need to worry." Her eyes canted down into his grocery cart. "Wow, that's a lot of frozen pizza."

He looked into his cart and saw he'd tossed probably ten frozen pizzas in there, along with an array of snacks. He shook his head and met her eyes again. "Not the best cook. Once fishing starts, I'll be eating a bit better. Then comes hunting season in the fall. Usually, I've got enough to make it through to summer, but my freezer died a few weeks ago," he offered with a rueful smile.

Jessa's eyes widened, alarmingly so. "You fish? And hunt?"

He nodded slowly. "I do. Hard to find anyone in Alaska who doesn't."

Jessa was quiet for a long moment. "Oh." She fiddled with the sleeve of her fleece jacket, twining it around her good hand. "I guess you don't get many vegetarians here, huh?"

Eli couldn't help but laugh as he shrugged. "Maybe a few. We get plenty of people visiting just because they like to fish and hunt though."

Jessa bit her lip, her teeth denting its plump softness and sending a jolt of awareness through him. "Oh. Well, I'm a vegetarian," She offered with a slight smile.

"There's plenty to do here that doesn't involve hunting and fishing, but I'd suggest you steer clear of the harbor when the boats are coming in."

"How come?"

"Because once fishing season starts, when the boats roll in, that means fish," he offered with a grin.

Jessa's return smile was wide and suddenly she burst into laughter. He didn't know what was so damn funny, but seeing her laugh just about made his day.

Available Now!

Stay With Me

Go here to sign up for information on new releases: http://jhcroixauthor.com/subscribe/

FIND MY BOOKS

Thank you for reading Falling Fast! I hope you enjoyed the story. If so, you can help other readers find my books in a variety of ways.

1) Write a review!

2) Sign up for my newsletter, so you can receive information about upcoming new releases & receive a FREE copy of one of my books: http://jhcroixauthor.com/subscribe/

3) Like and follow my Amazon Author page at https://amazon.com/author/jhcroix

4) Follow me on Bookbub at https://www.bookbub.com/authors/j-h-croix

5) Follow me on Twitter at https://twitter.com/JHCroix

6) Like my Facebook page at https://www.facebook.com/jhcroix

* * *

LAST FRONTIER LODGE NOVELS
Take Me Home

Love at Last
Just This Once
Falling Fast
Stay With Me
When We Fall
Hold Me Close
Crazy For You
Into The Fire Series
Burn For Me
Slow Burn
Burn So Bad
Hot Mess
Burn So Good
Sweet Fire
Play With Fire
Melt With You
Burn For You
Crash & Burn
Swoon Series
This Crazy Love
Wait For Me
Break My Fall
Brit Boys Sports Romance
The Play
Big Win
Out Of Bounds
Play Me
Naughty Wish
Diamond Creek Alaska Novels
When Love Comes
Follow Love
Love Unbroken
Love Untamed
Tumble Into Love
Christmas Nights

Catamount Lion Shifters
Protected Mate
Chosen Mate
Fated Mate
Destined Mate
A Catamount Christmas
Ghost Cat Shifters
The Lion Within
Lion Lost & Found

ACKNOWLEDGMENTS

A toast to my real-life hero who supports me in everything I do. Every book I write is made better by my editor, Laura Kingsley, so the thanks just keep on coming. Clarise Tan at CT Cover Creations is simply amazing when it comes to creating beautiful covers! Last, but never least: many, many thanks to my readers. Cheers to many more books ahead!

xoxo

J.H. Croix

ABOUT THE AUTHOR

USA Today Bestselling Author J. H. Croix lives in a small town in the historical farmlands of Maine with her husband and two spoiled dogs. Croix writes contemporary romance with sassy women and alpha men who aren't afraid to show some emotion. Her love for quirky small-towns and the characters that inhabit them shines through in her writing. Take a walk on the wild side of romance with her best-selling novels!

Places you can find me:
jhcroixauthor.com
jhcroix@jhcroix.com

www.ingramcontent.com/pod-product-compliance
Lightning Source LLC
Chambersburg PA
CBHW050512190726
48284CB00003B/780